"Boy!" she said. "You really know your Spanish, don't you?"

I looked around, pretending to be suddenly aware of her. Of course I'd long since noticed that she had immense brown eyes and arching eyebrows. And that she often seemed to be a bit surprised by what was going on. Even when she didn't know whatever she'd been asked, she didn't look embarrassed or distressed.

Now, up close, she dazzled me. Her skin was lightly tanned and totally unblemished. I had a sudden feeling of great tenderness. I would have liked to touch her, run my palm along her cheek and down her perfect little jawline. I wanted to protect her from all harm, and any dangers.

"Captures aspects of the high school scene perfectly— the cool guys; the jocks and cheerleaders; the teachers and administrators who don't have a clue; the uninvolved parents. . . . YAs will cheer for the happy ending." —*School Library Journal*

OTHER PUFFIN BOOKS YOU MAY ENJOY

JULIAN F. THOMPSON

Shepherd

PUFFIN BOOKS

*With many thanks to Douglas Hay
and Michael Lourie, who cheerfully
filled in some areas of ignorance.*

PUFFIN BOOKS
Published by the Penguin Group
Penguin Books USA Inc., 375 Hudson Street, New York, New York 10014, U.S.A.
Penguin Books Ltd, 27 Wrights Lane, London W8 5TZ, England
Penguin Books Australia Ltd, Ringwood, Victoria, Australia
Penguin Books Canada Ltd, 10 Alcorn Avenue, Toronto, Ontario, Canada M4V 3B2
Penguin Books (N.Z.) Ltd, 182–190 Wairau Road, Auckland 10, New Zealand

Penguin Books Ltd, Registered Offices: Harmondsworth, Middlesex, England

First published in the United States of America in 1993
by Henry Holt and Company Inc.
Published in Puffin Books, 1996

1 3 5 7 9 10 8 6 4 2

ISBN 0-14-037502-3

Printed in the United States of America

*For Polly, shepherd of my happiness,
and every other member of her flock.*

Shepherd

1

IN THE FIRST line of the Rolling Stones song "Sympathy for the Devil," Mick Jagger introduces himself as the Prince of Darkness and goes on to brag about all the history he was in on. I listen to a lot of classic rock. That surprises people, sometimes.

I'm not a devil, though. My theory is: If someone grows up on a farm, the way I have, the chances are he's not too devilish. That's not to say there aren't lunatics in rural areas. You bet there are. Sometimes they even make the pages of a magazine like *Time*, which I subscribe to, kids who do weird things with animals, or blow away their relatives with Pa's old double-barreled. But mostly, living on a farm, a person's apt to get—take on—a certain attitude, about the world in general. When you're farming, what you want to do is often not the reason you are doing such-and-such. The weather, or the season, or the cows decide. The things you do are things that *have to be* done then—which means you either get that certain attitude or you go nuts.

Accepting is the word that best describes the attitude that I'm referring to. Devils don't accept or go along with stuff. They're troublemakers. I am not a troublemaker.

Here's something else about myself. I have a grade-A memory for names, as well as other little facts. My uncle

Elbie told me once I maybe ought to take a shot at politics. To this day, I'm not completely sure if he was kidding.

"You shake hands good," was what he said to me that time, "and you remember everybody's name. On top of that, you're honest and you're ugly, which'll help to make the people trust you."

I knew a part of that was kidding. Don't get me wrong: I'd never brag that I was handsome. My face has certain chipmunk attributes that make me look . . . oh, less important and romantic than a truly handsome person does. But "ugly"? That's inaccurate; I'm telling you the truth. You can take my word for things, including how I look; Uncle Elbie's right about my honesty. Here's more: My skin's okay, although I'm not that tall; my hair is straight, dark brown and long, but not too long. I guess I *am* well-built. Of course, I could look better, but I also *could* look much, much worse. I could be, for instance, funny-looking.

But anyway, to continue. Let me illustrate my memory for names.

My name is Shepherd Catlett, known as Shep, and sometimes "Cats." I like my name all right; it's pretty cool. My uncle Elbie is a dairy farmer, like my dad, whose name is Darwin. Their farms are just a mile apart, both in the town of Burnside, although far from Burnside Center, where the high school that I go to is. Our land is over twenty miles from it, way up on Highridge Road. By accidental oversight, I forgot to say my mother's name is Laura. I am not a sexist.

Sometimes, kids at school will call us names—a name— the ten or twelve of us who come from way up Highridge Road. They call us "stumpjumpers." I say "ten or twelve" because there's two of us, the Delbert brothers, Dwight and Dwayne, who seldom make the bus. I don't care for being called a stumpjumper, even as a joke, and neither does Tara. But we don't make an issue out of it, even though it is unfair—ridiculous. That'd just encourage them to say it all the time.

Tara Garza and her mom are our near neighbors, and they always have been. She and I are eighteen days apart in age, and neither of us has a brother or a sister. We more or less grew up together, so we have the same opinions on a lot of things. Not everything, however. She has peculiar tastes in guys, the guys she dates, I think. But one thing we agree on is we're both as . . . sensitive as anyone from Burnside Center. Another is we both agree that Final Refuge is an awesome band.

But only one of us can hear—has heard—a message in a Final Refuge song.

The song is "Steam It Open," which is their second album's title track. It's a real old-fashioned rocker with a memorable chorus. ("Steam it open/ get the message/ Stop your hopin'/ learn the meaning/ Wholly written, wholly true/ The tricky part is known' what to do.")

I like a song that's got some content in it. But also isn't crystal-clear. "Steam It Open" is a song like that, a song that makes you think.

The part of it that's made me think the most, however, is the part that Tara and my mom can't hear, that no one hears, except for me, I'm pretty sure. It isn't in the verses or the chorus of the song. It comes in just as Bobbie Turnbull starts to play the bass part. A woman's voice that I don't recognize says, "Savor life." She doesn't sing it, she just says it.

Or that's what I believed she said, at first.

And I thought her saying that was pretty neat. I naturally

assumed it was a little quirky Final Refuge thing, handing out a piece of good advice, like that. Of course, I also thought, back then, that everyone could hear it. "Savor life." It seemed to me that neither I nor anyone I knew did that enough. Let's face it, life—not just my own, but in the sense of "every living thing"—is pretty precious and amazing, when you come to think about it.

Take, for instance: early morning in the summertime. The taste of good fresh milk. The way your dog will look at you, sometimes. How the smell of bacon hits your stomach. A breeze that carries clover blooming, or a grove of balsam fir.

"I really like it when she says that," I told Tara on the second day I had the tape.

"What?" she said. "When who says what?"

We were in my room at home. I stopped the tape deck and rewound a little ways, and played that part again.

"That," I said. "When she says, 'Savor life,' like that. Whoever she may be. I don't think it's someone in the band, do you? It doesn't really sound like Bobbie."

"You're telling me you just heard someone saying 'Savor life'?" said Tara.

I thought that she was kidding.

"Sure. Of course," I said.

"Play it one more time," she said, and so I did.

She listened, paused, then stared at me and flashed that sudden grin of hers.

"You didn't say you meant *subliminal*," she said. "Or that it was recorded *backwards*. I got it *that* time. Sure. Of course. That was the strangest thing, I swear, to get a sudden craving, just like that."

"A *craving*?" I inquired, thinking I was being kidded once again, but not exactly getting it.

6

"Of course," she said again. "For a Life Saver, right? In my case it was wint-o-green. Just yummy."

I smiled a sickly smile. Tara hadn't heard a thing. She thought that *I'd* been kidding *her*. I changed the subject.

Later on that night, I tried the tape out on my mom, telling her I'd read "some people" think they hear a voice in this one place on it. I played it twice for her (hearing "Savor life" myself, both times, as clear as anything), but she said no, that there was nothing *she* could hear.

"Of course," she said, "I *am* a little over thirty."

I decided that I might be having what I think is called an "auditory hallucination." It could have been brought on, I thought, by spending too long in the sun the day before, without a hat, when we were mending pasture fences. I figured when my brain cooled down, the words would fade away.

That didn't happen, though. The more I listened to the tape, the clearer it became, that woman's voice. Instead of fading, it got stronger. And, in about a week, I realized that it wasn't saying "Savor life" at all. The message was a lot more personal, I thought, but cruelly unspecific.

"Save *her* life" was what this honest, music-loving, not-bad-looking, *Time*-subscribing life-enjoying, farmer's son was being told to do.

2

I GUESS, at my age, no one ever really thinks he's crazy. Miserable, confused, incapable of functioning the way you're meant to, sure—but never crazy. It's only later on you learn what crazy is: miserable, confused, incapable of functioning the way you're meant to. Perhaps it crossed my mind that there was something wrong with me when I began to hear things on a Final Refuge tape that other people couldn't—or didn't, or wouldn't. But, if so, it was a passing thought; it didn't stick.

Remember that "accepting" riff of mine? The voice was something else that I accepted, but still there was one thing that bothered me about my hearing "Save her life" each time I played that tape. For the life of me, I couldn't figure out who "her" might be. None of the hers that I knew best seemed to be in any immediate danger. So what was I supposed to do? Read the want ads in the local paper? See if someone needed my left kidney, or the marrow of my bones?

I wished I could've talked to Tara, asked her what she thought my strategy should be.

Tara's very smart. Her memory is just about as sharp as mine, and she's also very good at putting facts together so's to come to a conclusion—which is what you have to do on essay questions, and in daily life, sometimes. She doesn't do that great in school because she says she has no reason to. In addition to her smartness, Tara knows me very, very well, as I have said before.

So, why didn't I talk to her? Get her to tell me what she thought was going on, and what I ought to do about it?

Well, I'd say that I was being ... prudent, taking care of something valuable. Put it this way: Tara's friendship's like a silver bowl my mother has, a bowl her many-times-great-grandfather made back in Connecticut, before the Revolutionary War. He was a silversmith, like Paul Revere, except I think he sided with the British. It isn't breakable, of course, but any time we use it, it is handled carefully, and not put down where accidents can happen to it.

I like the shape of our relationship—the one I have with Tara—just the way it is right now. No dents or scratches, anywhere. It'd be best if we could keep it as it is, I think. That's only common sense.

I'll say it one more time: I don't make trouble, or go looking for it, either.

We did, of course, continue to discuss a lot of other things, all sorts of different, common, everyday affairs.

"I'm completely screwed," she said to me, one evening on the phone. The voice was ten days old by then, still going strong.

"How so?" I asked.

"That weekend job I'm trying to get? Waitressing at Angela's, the fancy place in Dustin?"

"Um?" I said. Her latest boyfriend lived in Dustin. Probably you've heard of it; I think it's still the only town that's covered by a geodesic dome. But anyway, his name is Mitch, and he's a physician's assistant and twenty-eight years old.

Why would he want to date a seventeen-year-old (I asked myself)? And because I'd grown up on a farm, I'd known the answer to that question since about the age of five.

"Well, I told them I'd come after school tomorrow—they *interview* their girls, can you imagine?—and Emily had said she'd drive me over. But now it turns out her dumb *mother* needs the car. And Mom can't get off work, and I can't drive her car, even if I had a way to get to it, because of how they fouled up the insurance. I'm just *screwed*."

"Weep no more," I told her. "I promised *my* mom that I'd take *her* car to school one day this week, so I could get to Dustin after and pick up a lamp she left there to get fixed. I bet tomorrow's perfectly all right with her. I'll take you there and bring you back for . . . oh, say, ten percent of all your tips, assuming that you get the job. How 'bout it? Deal?" Angela's was the most expensive restaurant in Dustin, and everything in Dustin costs a fortune, since the dome went up.

"Don't tease," she said. "You know how much I'm counting on this job, the money from this job."

I could guess how Tara looked, while she was saying that. There are certain things she gets intense about, and when she does, her dark brows draw together, and she winds a strand of hair from right beside her ear around her middle finger. Money is a thing that she gets *real* intense about, these days.

Tara's short, about five-three, but not a reed, no wispy little thing; she's solid. And she's got the most amazing face. *I* think she looks like some kind of warrior princess from another place and time; her features are all dark and clear and strong, but also sensitive and feminine—*distinguished*, you could say. Her hair is very nearly black and surely is a mane. I can imagine her on horseback, armored but bare-legged, sword in hand, that black mane like a banner as she leads her troops into the fray. Going just by looks, I guess I would have been a member of her infantry, scurrying along on foot, beside her.

Anyway, I sure know all about what Tara wanted money for. She had this monomania: She felt she needed to escape, not just from Highridge Road, but out of Burnside altogether.

"*You* know what I mean," she'd said to me the year before. "I notice *you've* made plans to split, go off and live up at the university. And *you* say you don't even mind it here."

I told her that was true, all that. I didn't bring up how I'd kept on wishing that she'd come to college with me—what a huge and scary step this going off to college seemed to me to be. Long since, she'd made it clear to me that her mother didn't have the money, any money, for her college education, and I'd accepted that. Well, on the surface, anyway. My parents told me that her father'd split for parts unknown the day that she was born. He'd heard it was a girl, and then had driven out of town, my mother said.

Now I said (to change the subject), "Well, my mother was a waitress once, and she said she averaged a proposal every two weeks. You may not ever need the bucks you make at Angela's. You may meet some zillionaire in there, and marry him, and move to California, *I* don't know."

"Are you sure your mother didn't say 'a *proposition*,' Cats?" she asked.

When I got to Tara's house, next morning, her mother walked her to the car, carrying the dress that Tara planned to wear to Angela's that afternoon.

"It's great that you can do this, Shep," her mother said to me. "You've really saved her life, you know."

Doink. I stared at her. And then I must have looked at Tara strangely after she had gotten in beside me. I know it's rude to stare.

"Shepherd?" she inquired. And she snapped her fingers twice, about eye-level. "You forgotten something? Have I got a cornflake on my tooth?"

"No, no," I said, and put the Buick into gear. And, "Sorry. It was just . . . my mind was somewhere else."

Where it was was back at home, of course. I couldn't wait to get back there and play the tape. Had I "saved her life," as Mrs. Garza'd said? Was *that* what I was meant to do?

Tara was inside of Angela's for forty minutes, and she came out beaming. They'd given her a tryout, made her write some orders down and carry a big heavy tray with spilly stuff on it, and everything. At the end, they'd told her she was hired and could count on eighty bucks a night, and twice or even three times that when things were really busy—as they often were. Tara was ecstatic.

"I can make a month's rent in a *weekend*, Shep," she told me.

That was so strange to think of, Tara in her own apartment, paying rent, and living in a city. Acceptable, I guess, if that was what she wanted, but still strange.

When I played the tape, it still was there, as loud and clear as ever: "Save her life." So my assumption was, I hadn't done it yet, whatever it might be. What Tara's mother'd said had just been an . . . *expression*. And, of course, a huge exaggeration.

Well, that's good, I thought. If I was going to hear things, maybe *do* things, I was good for more than that, I hoped. I mean, I might not be Mel Gibson, but come on.

3

THE WEEKEND after that, I had the house all to myself on Saturday, from after second milking on. My parents had left about five-thirty; they were driving to the lake—Lake Breen—where they'd stay overnight with friends, returning at the crack of dawn on Sunday. Ben Murchison, who helps my dad, had headed homeward to his trailer, which was three miles farther out, on Highridge Road.

Although it was a Saturday, I didn't have a date. I hadn't tried to get one. No real reason, does there have to be?

I do go out. Girls *will* go out with me. I'm not an outcast, an untouchable, far from it. But it's also fair to say my popularity is . . . limited. I don't imagine that will change. If I became a group, they'd never book me in a stadium.

I don't know which aspect of myself would be my biggest limitation, when it comes to girls. It's possibly my looks; I'm sure they play a part. I have those chipmunk cheeks, and my blue eyes are not enormous; in fact, they get a little *slitty* when I smile. It also wouldn't hurt at all if I could grow, be taller than my present five foot ten, or if I had a more assertive jaw, or a beard. To be completely fair, I also ought to say that *Tara* told me once I had "lead singer's looks"—the "fresh-faced, beardless-boy variety" (I memorized those words, and more). "If I managed you," she said, "I'd have you up there wearing, like, a football jersey, cropped, and with the sleeves cut off, so the girls could see the muscles on your biceps and your belly. And when their mothers saw your poster, they'd go, 'Why can't all the others look like *him*?'" Tara said that kind of stuff, but that was Tara. She was more like family; you couldn't trust her compliments.

Besides my looks, I have some other problems. I'm not a natural for any of the major cliques at school. There isn't any *slot* just waiting there for me, someplace where I fit in.

If I was different than I am, and a member of some group or clique, I either would have had a date that night or been going to a party that a fellow jock (or prep, or greaser) asked me to, where I might see somebody and begin a new relationship with them. You know how that works. At parties, sometimes people get to talking, even dancing, with some kid they've seen around for years, but never really talked to. And they find they like the same shows on TV, or things to eat, or singers, even teachers, and before you know it, bingo!—a relationship is born. A guy like me plods into someone's house, alone, and when he dances out of there, four hours later, he is with his brand-new girlfriend. Who might be someone younger, cute, like Mary Sutherland. That hasn't happened to yours truly, but I'm sure it happens. *Pretty* sure. Well, doesn't it?

I know that Tara meets these older guys, like Mitch, up at the hospital, where she and Emily are aides. I guess it's true that you can pick up things at hospitals.

So, instead of heading out that night, or having people over, I prepared to spend some time alone, to "entertain myself," as Mom suggested I do all the time, when I was younger. Over the years, I'd gotten good at that. Being by myself was super-fine with me.

I started out by sitting on the porch, with music playing on the tape deck in the living room, turned way up, and the windows and the French door open. Included in the tapes I'd brought down from my room was "Steam It Open." I hadn't heard it coming from my parents' speakers yet, and that was something I'd been looking forward to. I always like to have things that I'm looking forward to.

It was fantastic; I enjoyed it to the max, the voice and all. But before half an hour passed, I started getting hungry. The second item on the schedule I'd planned was "Eat."

Setting up a schedule was typical. It's another thing that farmers do, even though they know their "best laid plans" can get messed up real easily, and often do. My schedule for that afternoon and evening was: Listen to some music; eat; sit outside and watch the darkness fall; go inside and see the Movie of the Week on television.

The menu that my mom and I'd agreed upon was home fries, turkey franks, and salad, with a brownie and some frozen yogurt for dessert.

Here's the way to make a batch of Shepherd Catlett home fries (and the rest of that night's dinner). Believe me, it is worth the trouble.

First, get out a skillet—also called a frying pan, by some—a big black iron one, if possible. Into it you put your butter, two or three fat pats' worth, followed by a little pour of cooking oil (canola oil, at home). Turn the burner on, to where the dial says "medium," and while the butter's melting, quickly slice three onions pretty thin and toss the slices in the skillet—after sizzling the grease around a little. Cover.

Next, locate the four cold baked potatoes that your mother

swore were in the fridge, and slice *them* up, not so thinly. (Baked potatoes are a key ingredient. Don't try using raw ones; they're a different story altogether. *Silas Marner* compared to . . . I don't know, *The Old Man and the Sea*, I guess.)

As you cut the spuds, keep checking on your onions. Each time you do so, flip them casually around the skillet. I use a spatula for that, so they don't stick. I want those onion slices to be golden-brown, not burned, not yet. That will happen— just to some of them—but later, at the end.

(Oh, I should have said I put a pot of water on to boil, as soon as I get in the kitchen, if I'm having turkey franks. I generally eat five of them, with ketchup, not on buns. When the water boils, I drop the franks in, let the water boil again, slap a cover on *that* pot, and turn its burner off. In seven minutes they'll be swollen, steaming hot, and super-edible. And they'll stay that way until you've got your home fries ready.)

When the onions reach that golden-brown I spoke of, layer potato slices right on top of them and sprinkle the whole deal with salt and quite a lot of pepper. If there's a pepper grinder handy, use it; it'll give you better pepper. Then cover up the skillet once again.

After about a minute, take your spatula and turn the onions and potatoes. You don't have to do that neatly. In fact, it's good to mix them up together, some; the idea is to get some grease and onion bits on each potato slice. Feel free to add more butter if the contents of the pan look dry or stick excessively; home fries *want* to be a little greasy. When the mixture's good and hot (about four stirrings later), some onion slices should be slightly burned, and some potato pieces will be brown. And if you haven't fainted dead away from hunger, you are smiling and your mouth is watering;

don't try to talk. You've made yourself some Shepherd Cat-lett home fries. Yum.

Scrape your fries onto a serving platter, then drain the franks and spear a couple, making sure the ketchup's handy. I suggest: a big green salad on the side (my mother always leaves said greens all washed and in a plastic bag), a glass of milk nearby, and that you only put the ketchup on the franks; the fries are perfect as they are. Then let the games begin. For fifteen minutes, silence should be broken only by the sound of chewing, and of knife and fork on tableware, by swallows and contented sighs.

When I'd finished eating all the fries and franks and salad, I took the pot, the skillet, the platter, and the bowl across the kitchen to the sink and washed them (I am *not* a trouble-maker), and extracted one large brownie from the pan inside the cupboard. On top of it, I slopped some frozen yogurt (berry-swirl, this time), and took the bowl back to the porch. I could have dessert *and* watch the darkness fall, together. Good idea. I didn't need to have the music on at this point. I like to listen to the twilight world, as well as watch it.

There was just one bite of brownie left when I first heard the little bleating sound. By then, it was gray dusk. I didn't know what I was hearing. I also didn't know where it was coming from. Down the road a little ways, I thought, possibly across the road, as well. My curiosity was piqued. I like to know what's going on.

The noise was nothing like a dog's whine or a cat's meow. It made me think a little of a baby sheep or goat, but no one I could think of had a lamb or kid that might have gotten loose. It was *not* a catbird, if you've thought of that.

Oh, well (I thought). I ate the brownie bite and glanced down at my watch. It was almost time to turn on the TV. The

Movie of the Week was *Mystic Pizza*. I was pretty sure that it had Julia Roberts in it. That Mary Sutherland I mentioned? She could have been Ms. Roberts's younger sister.

But as I started off the porch, heading for the big French doors, my bowl in my untroublemaking hand, I heard the sound once more. It got to me this time. It touched not just my country curiosity, but also other aspects of my nature. One other aspect, anyway. Let's not get into giving it a name.

I didn't need a princess warrior to lead me. I went into the house and got a flashlight, then came back and started down the road. Of course the bleating sound had stopped by then; the dusky world was silent.

The place that I was heading for was not that far away, my mother's ex-asparagus patch. Some years before—like, six or eight—my mother had decided that she wanted fresh asparagus, home-grown. She'd gotten Ben to till a little plot for her, and put a chicken-wire fence around it, and she'd fertilized and seeded it.

Well, asparagus takes time. You don't just plant some seeds and eat some spears that year; asparagus *evolves*. Mother either hadn't realized that or had forgotten. She got annoyed at the asparagus and said to heck with it. The second year the plot was overgrown with weeds; then brush, including briars, grew in there. Last time I noticed, there were one or two nice maple shoots. The chicken wire sagged and rusted.

I didn't make an effort to go quietly. In fact, and to the contrary, I'm pretty sure I whistled, going down the road. If whatever it had been had moved along, why, that was perfectly all right with me. But I kept on going, heart and all.

It wasn't fully dark. You still saw shapes and outlines, just no details; the patch was all in shadow, though. I flicked the flashlight on and waved the beam around.

When the light first hit the thing, its rounded back, I gasped and thought (don't laugh), "My God, it's a hyena!" I think the reason for that was that I'd watched a nature show about the Serengeti Plain the week before, and it had had hyenas in it. Of course I'd never seen one in the flesh. I *thought* I'd seen a catamount one time, but never a hyena.

And I wasn't looking at one then. As soon as what was there picked up its head and started struggling, I realized it was a spotted fawn, tangled in—held captive by—that rusty chicken-wire fencing. I let my breath out slowly and began to mumble at the thing, the way we farmers do to animals, particularly animals in trouble. The words are unimportant, I believe; it's the tone of voice that counts.

I hesitated, standing just outside the garden plot. The little deer did not respond (at once, or ever) to the soothing sounds that I was making; it was really messed up in that wire. Instead of standing still, it sort of panicked, bleating once again and throwing its small body back and forth, this way and that, trying to get free. I was afraid that it would hurt itself, those little pipe-stem legs they have.

I knew there were some wire cutters somewhere in my father's shop, up near the barn, but I didn't know if I could find them right away. And I didn't want to leave the fawn alone too long. If there were coyotes anywhere around—we have them in these hills these days—they'd soon be coming to investigate. Baby deer are home fries to those guys.

I decided I would try to free the fawn bare-handed.

You'd think it wouldn't have been that hard, considering the size and weight of each of us, but Jiminy, it was. In the end, I had to take the flannel shirt that I'd been wearing and envelop her in it. Then I held her up against my chest as best I could, kneeling down beside her while I tried to free those sharp-toed little hooves. Fear gave her strength and quickness I could not believe. I've handled calves a lot, but they're like teddy bears, I promise you, compared to how that little deer was.

But finally she was loose and scampering away, unharmed as far as I could tell. If coyotes were around, I didn't hear them, either then or when I got back up there to the porch, to set a minute. I was muddy, grass-stained, briar-whipped, and out of breath; two fingers had small wire cuts on them. I decided that I'd better change my schedule and take a shower next. I was going to miss a lot of *Mystic Pizza*, but I accepted that, all right. I was happy that I'd done what I had done.

Slowly, then, it sunk in what that was. Possibly—no, probably, and no exaggeration this time—I had . . . saved her life.

I took my shower then, and watched the last half of the movie; it was good. But before I went to bed, I had to play the "Steam It Open" tape again. Don't ask what I was hoping; some of each, I think.

The voice was just as loud and clear as ever, down there in the living room, coming through my parents' much, much better speakers.

"Save her life," I still was being told.

This is getting just a bit ridiculous, I thought. But I didn't think that *angrily,* at all.

4

I T I S N ' T definite that I am going to be a farmer, after college. Not at all. I don't feel a lot of pressure from my parents, I don't think—not on *this* issue, anyway—even as the only son, the only *child*.

Uncle Elbie has four robust, cheerful boys, aged six through twelve, all of whom are heavy into Tonka toys. It isn't like the land will leave the family, or get developed, if I head into banking, or become a politician, say.

My dad says this: "It's not for everyone, a farmer's life." He also says, "But if you like it, you can't beat it."

As of now, I like it but I may not love it. If you *love* it, you can't beat it, probably. But liking it and loving it are poles apart. I think you have to *marry* farming. It seems to me I need to go on lots more dates, before I settle down.

"Boy, this sure does take a lot of energy," I said, the third morning after the evening of the home fries and the fawn. It was 5:15 A.M., and all our milking machines were going, drawing milk from eight cows at a time, and sending it through plastic tubes to the big stainless steel tank in the milk house. My father and I were standing side by side, dressed alike in rubber boots and coveralls, and enjoying everything going right, or seeming to, for the moment. Ben was doing likewise, but across from us, behind the other row of cows.

"What, standing here?" my father said. "Folding both your arms like that? Thinking up something you want to say?" He likes to practice being funny sometimes. He's forty-two, and in terrific shape, except for being more than halfway bald—I wonder if I've got *that* gene. He always wears a cap except inside the house, but so does almost every man on Highridge Road.

"No, of course not," I replied, ignoring his auroral humor. "I meant the whole business of milk production. Not that it isn't worth it. But when I think of all we spend a month for electricity and diesel fuel—how much of both we have to use—it's just disgusting."

"Sure does take a bite of every milk check," he agreed.

"Well, actually," I said, "what I was thinking of was the environment. All the fossil fuels that we burn up, indirectly and directly. And what that's doing to the atmosphere, to the future of the planet."

"You know what's worse?" my father said. "A jumbo jet. I bet you we could run this farm for a couple of *years* on what it takes to fly a jumbo jet from Boston to the Caribbean, and then back again. One time." He noticed that a cow was done and went to move the apparatus over one.

The reason I had brought up global warming was that recently I'd started focusing upon another female life I thought I ought to save: the planet's, Mother Earth's. The goddess of the earth was Gaia, back in ancient Greece (example of my memory for names), and I'd decided it was time I helped her out. It was pretty depressing to see how apathetic lots of people were, or selfish, people my own age. So I decided I'd become a very minor activist, hard as that'd be for me to do. I don't like to call attention to myself. I guess I've made it clear I'm not an entertainer, like a Willie Nelson is, or Jackson Browne.

What I did was work obliquely, through some people who had power. For instance, I convinced our high-school principal that paper waste in school could easily be separated, and lots of it recycled, not just burned. Art teachers started letting kids make posters on environmental themes (at my suggestion). I had a meeting with the mother who was head of the PTA, which resulted in their planting trees around the edges of the school property, instead of paying for a giant new electric football scoreboard.

Small stuff, all that, I grant you, but consider the source. You do what you are able to. I'm also not Ralph Nader, or a Jacques Cousteau.

Riding on the bus to school on Monday morning, I mentioned that PTA business to Tara, thinking that she might be pleased. She believes too much is made of football at our school; violence, even in a padded uniform, is not acceptable to Tara. I'm a guy; I watch the Giants on TV.

She reacted, but not as I'd expected.

"Mrs. Vail was at the restaurant on Friday night," she said. Mrs. Vail was Mrs. PTA, the woman I'd talked to. "Not at any of my tables, though, thank God. Doris told me that her husband had this pocket calculator with him that he used to figure out the tip. Fifteen percent *exactly*, to the nickel! He made her bring an extra dollar of his change in *coins*, so's to be sure he wouldn't overtip. Can you imagine that?"

I clucked and shook my head, denoting sympathy for Doris.

"So, how did *you* make out?" I asked. "You wear your lucky blouse again?"

Tara smiled and nodded, looking down. I think she possibly regretted telling me about that blouse, a pretty low-cut one she'd gone and got in hopes that it would bring her "luck."

The deal was: Waitresses at Angela's all wear white blouses and black pants, which they supply. But if you want to, you can bring your own, and the restaurant will pay your cleaning bills. It also must approve your outfit, in advance.

"They wouldn't want you *hanging out,*" Tara'd said to me. "And anyway, that wouldn't be intelligent. Like Doris said, you want to get the gentlemen to notice you, while not exactly *challenging* the ladies." Since then, I'd tried imagining how Tara'd look in that white blouse, while setting down a slice of cantaloupe, let's say. The verdict, every time, was *excellent.*

"I had a good night Friday," Tara told me now. "Not a great night, but real good. Saturday was great. Between the two, I made three hundred bucks almost. And they hardly laid a hand on me, all night."

"What?" I said. I raised my eyebrows, made a pincers of my hand, and waggled it before her eyes. I sort of had convinced myself that wasn't something that the clientele at Angela's—guys in coats and ties with silver hair—would do.

"Oh, they don't *pinch* us," Tara said. "They're much more . . . subtle. Being from the country, up on Highridge Road, you may not know the phrase, the slang expression, 'cop a feel'? Can you *imagine* what that might refer to?"

"Well, let me think," I said. I did my best to sound like Woody Boyd on *Cheers.* "I've seen a lot of *fields,* of course. And, naturally, I'm into *cobs,* if you mean corn cobs. So, 'cob a field' would mean . . ." I shook my head and crinkled up my eyebrows. "No, I guess I just don't know, Miss Garza."

Tara sighed. "It mostly happens when they're leaving," she explained. "They're thanking you for taking such good care of them—the tip's already history—and then they put a hand around your waist and let it go slip-sliding, up *or* down. They can make it all seem very accidental, if they're any good at it."

I shook my head again.

"As far as they're concerned," she said, "we're almost asking for it—or expect it, anyway. Or we wouldn't take a job like that." She shrugged. "But I'll say this: They pay a lot for what they get. And it isn't all of them. Besides, there's lots worse things than being pawed a little."

She shifted slightly in her seat. Her head of jet-black hair was now a fraction higher than my own, it seemed. It was as if she'd raised herself above it all.

I shrugged, myself, and chewed on what she'd said. The big banana of a school bus we were on kept cruising down the road. In one respect, that didn't sound like Tara, what she'd said. Since we'd been old enough to talk (a little, some) about that kind of stuff, she'd never seemed too tolerant of guys who . . . well, *presumed* too much. In fact, though this may give you the idea that I'm meek or out of it, I'd sort of based the way *I* acted with a girl on what I thought I'd learned from Tara—how she seemed to feel a boy *should* act. I had to wonder if I'd possibly misread her.

Of course it also *could* be she was being stoical—not whiny. When Tara wanted something, she'd put up with inconvenience and unpleasantness to get it. Having been brought up on Highridge Road, Tara'd learned to . . . well, *accept things*, too.

"I guess with the experience you'll have," I said, "you probably could get a job at some big restaurant in Boston." She turned her head to look at me. "I mean, next year. That's *if* you wanted to."

Probably she knew that I was fishing, trying to find out what kind of stuff she planned to *do,* once she'd made her dream come true and gotten clean away from Burnside, and from Highridge Road.

Chances are she also knew what else I had in mind, which was that now that she was making all this money, maybe she should reevaluate the college option.

It was clear (at least to me) that this job of hers changed everything. If she kept it for the whole school year, she would have *thousands* in the bank by summertime. And if she slashed her Mitch-time to the minimum, or even cut it out, and studied in those hours (as well as on the bus, both ways, and in the evening), she'd be making A's in all her courses, I just knew she would. That'd mean she'd be in line for maximum financial aid, and wouldn't have to take that big a loan. Almost before she blinked, we'd be together on the college green up there, looking at a map and trying to figure out if "that one" was the library!

What made this so completely logical and *smart* (to me) was that it filled—and in a far, far better way than Boston did—what Tara called her "need" to get away from home.

"When I say 'need,'" she'd told me once, "I speak of something on the order of, say, *oxygen,* or food and water, shelter, sleep. I doubt that you believe me, Shep; maybe what I'm saying isn't credible to you. But this is a survival issue, understand? You haven't got a clue of what it's like for me to live with Mom these days." And yes, she'd wound her hair around her finger during that.

I'd nodded, making myself look agreeable (I thought), but it was true—I didn't altogether understand. Tara's mom would not have been a first-round pick of mine, if I'd been making choices in some Desert Island League, but still; she never seemed *that* bad. But when I'd offered that opinion, Tara shook her mane around.

"You never see—or *hear*—that side of her," she'd said. "But it's the stuff I have to listen to, day after day. All she ever does is bitch—about her job, about the house, about the people in this town, how petty and how boring they all are, except for one or two." She'd heaved a major sigh. "I ask her why she doesn't leave. I've *begged* her to just sell the house and move. I've even told her I'd go with her, gladly, if she'd move to someplace she admitted that she *liked*."

"What does she say to that?" I'd asked.

"Oh, she says it's not that easy," Tara'd said. "That people can't find work, start fresh again, at her age. That with the housing market like it is right now, we'd have to almost give our place away. And besides, she says, the cities are too dangerous, and she wouldn't know a living soul, et cetera, et cetera."

Well, that had ended *that* attempt of mine to understand her situation. But now there was this new thing that she had to answer to: my not-so-subtle waitressing-in-Boston question, which was not a question, really.

Tara fixed me with a look and very slowly said the following: "All I want is for the time to pass so that it gets to *be* next year. And I am living in my own apartment, on my own, in Boston. When that's happened, you can call me up—I imagine there's a pay phone on each corridor, in all those college dorms—and *ask* me what I'm doing. Up until that time"— she jabbed an elbow in my ribs—"remember the old saying,

Shep." She painted on a wicked grin. " 'Curiosity kills the Catlett.' "

I grunted, smiled a little sourly, and reached inside my backpack for *King Lear*. I thought that I was feeling like the mad old monarch in the play, pierced by a (different) set of attitudes that felt as bad or worse than snakebites.

But I wasn't going to point out what was surely obvious to her (as well as me) about the money, or the value of an education. Nor was I going to burden her with what were, after all, *my* fears and needs. They wouldn't kill me; I would learn to live with them. I didn't have a choice, that I could see.

5

I KNOW I've mentioned the name Mary Sutherland a time or two. The girl who *I* think could be Julia Roberts's younger sister, going by her looks? She's just a freshman, three whole years behind me in school.

I think it's funny about men's and women's ages. My dad is four years older than my mom, and Uncle Elbie's eight years older than Aunt May. I'm sure that no one jumped up at their weddings to complain that those two men were getting set to tie the knot with girls who were too young for them. I bet you no one even *thought* that that was so. My mom was twenty, after all, and my aunt May a ripe old twenty-one.

But if a boy is seventeen and starts to go with someone who is almost *fifteen*, hey, look out! Certain people start right in on him, as if he's evil, or pathetic, or perverted; honestly, I've seen that happen. They say the girl is "much too young for him." Everybody thinks that he, the boy, is simply out "to take advantage of" the girl (or "just looking for one thing"), and that she, the girl, is much too immature to know "what she is getting into."

Because I knew all that, it never crossed my mind to try to go with Mary Sutherland. Or, wait; that isn't being honest. It certainly *did* cross my mind—in fact, almost as frequently as deer cross Highridge Road to get to the alfalfa growing on Hay Flats. But I was wary, on account of all this age stuff that I knew. And because of other factors, like the likelihood that she'd be totally uninterested in me, at any age. Face it, my main claim to fame—that I get decent grades in school and score well on the SATs—doesn't even seem to grab the other members of my class who also make a lot of A's. I think *they* think I just get lucky on the tests. No, what I figured was: Any chance I had with Mary Sutherland would come as a result of . . . oh, my saving her from drowning, or a burning building, maybe. I never thought of Spanish I in that regard.

But that was how we came to know each other. By great good luck (or "fate," as later on I thought it was) *I* was in her Spanish class—yes, Spanish I, first-year or beginner's Spanish!

I didn't sign up for the class because of Mary Sutherland. When I signed up for it, last spring, I didn't know that she existed. It was an idea my guidance counselor, my parents, and I came up with. I'd taken my three years of French already; I had a knack for languages; Spanish could be useful in the future (there are lots of cows in South America, I guess); compared to all the other courses on my schedule, it should be a breeze. Mary Sutherland was like the gift inside a box of Cracker Jacks.

(Don't misunderstand that, please. I meant that in the sense of being something extra, over and above what you were mainly after, to begin with. I *never* thought of her as being like a *toy,* or something cheap or silly that you'd give or throw away. That wouldn't be like me at all, thinking of a girl that way.)

Anyway, I was the only full-fledged senior they enrolled in Spanish I, but not the only Highridge Roader. Dwayne Delbert had signed up for it, apparently; from time to time, the first few weeks, he'd make a cameo appearance. When Señora Markham asked if he had done the homework, Dwayne would always laugh and say, *"Mañana."* He laughed a lot when people spoke to him. It was as if he just assumed that everyone was joking. Based on age, I think he should have been a senior, but in terms of graduation credits, who knows what he was? Some computer and his guidance counselor, I guess.

Dwayne and his younger brother Dwight, they'd hardly missed a day of school when they were younger. I was friendly with them then. Not that I'm not now; we just don't talk that much, the way we used to. They liked to fish, the same as me, and we would talk about how many we caught where, and about what pool we hooked the biggest trout we'd ever seen in.

It was in junior high they started to pull back, go off with just each other. Dwayne got a bluetick hound that he began to train at night, and so I guess he slept in lots of days. Dwight was not inclined to go to school without him. Now Dwayne was also into hunting turkeys. Sometimes I'd see him at the Highridge Corners Store in turkey season. He'd be dressed in camouflage from top to toe, even have his face and hands all painted up, in blacks and browns and greens. One day he brought his turkey call onto the bus and practiced gobbling in there till Mrs. Bates, the driver, yelled at him to stop before she came back there and pecked him in the head. He laughed at that one, too, but did what he was told. He was an easygoing sort of kid, I'd say.

Anyway, because we had that Spanish class together, it was natural or even, you could say, inevitable that one day Mary Sutherland and I would be beside each other as we left the classroom. In fact, that didn't happen till the last day of the fifth whole week of school. And it was she who spoke to *me*.

"Boy!" she said. "You really know your Spanish, don't you?"

I looked around, pretending to be suddenly aware of her. Of course I'd long since noticed that she had immense brown eyes and arching eyebrows. And that she often seemed to be a bit surprised by what was going on. Even when she didn't know whatever she'd been asked, she didn't look embarrassed or distressed.

Now, up close, she dazzled me. Her skin was lightly tanned and totally unblemished. I had a sudden feeling of great tenderness. I would have liked to touch her, run my palm along her cheek and down her perfect little jawline. I wanted to protect her from all harm, and any dangers.

"Not really," I replied. "I'm strictly a beginner, just like you. I did take French before, though." I fell in step beside her, going down the hall. I hoped she wouldn't run. She had a soft gray sweater on; there was a thin gold chain around her neck. Her breasts were flattened by the notebooks she held clutched in both her arms. She swayed a little as she walked; her slender body was cut high, with legs as long as mine almost. I smelled a clean, light fragrance, as if she'd come from showering, instead of out of Spanish class.

"Maybe that's it, then," she said. "That you know French already. You've got an awesome Spanish accent. You sound like Ms.—I mean *Señora*—Markham." She giggled, wrinkling her nose. I snuck a hand into a pocket, gave myself a pinch; she was being friendly! "Except Señora's *Mrs.*, isn't it? The Spanish got a word for *Ms.*, you think?"

"I don't know," I said. "But if you want to work on your pronunciation—like, your Spanish accent—they have some tapes down at the resource center you can use. I've been doing that; they really help."

Señora Markham had suggested it, of course. In fact, she'd

mentioned listening to tapes at some point during almost every class. Still, Mary's eyebrows went up higher when she heard that I'd been using them. But, almost right away, she shook her head.

"Mrs. Blaylock doesn't like me," she explained. Mrs. B. was the librarian. "She yelled at me the second day of school." Her round, wet lower lip stuck out a little farther. "She's a mean old biddy. All I was trying to do was find out an assignment."

She looked up, straight into my eyes, and smiled this slightly mad, completely mischievous, *enormous* smile of hers. Now that I thought of it, I'd *noticed* Mrs. Blaylock could be crabby sometimes; I thought that probably those young kids Mary's age were getting to be too much for her, with all their curiosity, and energy.

"Maybe you could be my tapes," she said to me. "You could say the words from the ... vo-cabel-*aire*o"—that smile again—"then I could say them back. And you could, like, correct me."

This was amazing. She wanted me to help her, spend some time with her, be her *buen amigo*.

"I could try," I said. Then, being honest, being *stupid*: "But my accent's far from perfect. I might not do you any good at all, you know. The tapes are much—"

She waved the tapes away with her left hand; it had a ring on every finger but the middle one. "I'd rather put my faith in you," she said, and smiled at me a third time. "So, beginning when?"

"After school sometime would probably be the best," I said. "I've got a pretty heavy schedule, right now." My dad had said that school activities had first priority, before the chores I'd do around the barn when I was able to, when I got home. This might stretch the meaning of *activities* a bit, I thought, but not too much. Or anyway, too often. Besides, at seventeen, I had to have a *life* apart from classes, cows, and family; I wasn't any hired *man*.

She was nodding. "Yeah, I've seen the books and stuff you lug around." Her eyes went on a trip behind me, to my pack, I guess. "What are you, anyway, a junior?"

"No," I said, "a senior. I'm a real old man." I had a flash of gladness Tara wasn't listening to this, this conversation I was having with the freshman Mary Sutherland.

"Lucky you," she said. And then, excitedly, "So how about on *Monday*—after school? Is it a date?" She made it sound like . . . I don't know. But something better than a study session. Something more along the lines of *fun*. In class, she'd never seemed to get excited over Spanish.

"Okay," I said. "The one thing is, I'll have to just make sure that I can get a car. I don't live right here in town."

"Oh, you mean you take the bus most days? You go home on a *bus*?" She made that sound absurd, impossible—like "spacecraft."

"Uh-huh." I could feel myself . . . well, *shrivel*.

"To where? How far?" she asked. "You live a long way from the Center? I don't think that I could stand it, if I had to get a bus to school. I'd feel so out of it, not being close to . . . *you* know, everything. Where *do* you live, exactly?"

"Out Highridge Road a ways," I said. There wasn't any point in getting angry. "If you know where that is."

"*Highridge* Road?" You would have thought I'd said the planet Jupiter. "Isn't that all farms and stuff?"

"A-yup," I said. I thought: Why not the whole nine yards? This wasn't going to work at all. "I live on a dairy farm. My name's Shep Catlett." There wasn't any point in telling her I was . . . who? *Bon Jovi?*

"The same as Catlett *Dairies*?" Her tone changed altogether, to one of pleasure and amazement. Now I felt as if I was a long-lost relative of hers. "My mom gets *milk* from you, can you believe it? The kind with *cream* on top!"

"Well, actually, that comes from Uncle Elbie's place," I said. "Most of ours ends up in those big tanker trucks, the ones with 'Agri-Mark' all over them? You may have seen them here in town."

She nodded, vaguely. "Oh, yeah," she said. She looked at me more carefully, I thought. More coolly and judgmentally, perhaps. Comparing me with someone else, no doubt. My looks, primarily, I guess.

"You don't look a whole lot like a farmer," she said finally. "Living on a farm, that must be weird." She shook her head, then quickly brightened. "Cows are cool, though," she opined. "Especially the black and white ones."

We'd gotten to the place where our corridor dead-ended, and you had to take a left or right.

"Which way you going?" Mary asked.

"Right." I jerked my head. "I've got a lab."

"I go the other way," she said. I wasn't in the least surprised. But she went on. "So, we got a date? Like, meet me on the steps out front, on Monday after school?"

"Okay," I said. "And if I can't round up a car, I'll let you know in class."

"Cool," she said, and smiled a final time, and flicked her fingers out at me as she turned and headed down the hall. I watched her for a second, watched that little hip sway, how her round (but slender) butt went left and right; the rest of her just floated.

I managed to procure my mother's car, all right, telling her there was some extra stuff I had to do for Spanish; I planned to say the same to Tara when I picked her up and drove her down to school that day. I hoped there wouldn't be a question period.

I felt a little guilty, burning gasoline, a fossil fuel, for such a purpose. If there was a next time, maybe I'd hitch home. If things worked out just right, I never would get into just what kind of "extra stuff" it was I had to do—either with my mom or Tara. Mom's curiosity, when it came to any aspect of my social life, was absolutely boundless; she could make me feel like some old sugar maple with a half a dozen taps in it sometimes. Tara might not know what Mary looked like, but she'd demand a name from me, and shortly she'd find out. Maybe she'd be what a good friend *should* be—totally supportive, deeply understanding—but there *was* a chance of maybe not. Tara sometimes liked to tease, and more than anybody else's teasing, hers could get to me.

My helping Mary wasn't any of her business, really. There was nothing "going on," and nothing *would* "go on"; I wasn't going to kid myself. Why have to listen to a lot of jokes, all based on someone's false assumptions?

I saw Mary in our class on Monday morning, but I didn't get a chance to talk with her. She left the room before me, surrounded by three girlfriends; by the time I reached the hall, they'd disappeared.

She wasn't anywhere outside the front part of the school that afternoon, after the last period. Not *on* the steps, above, below, or off to either side of them. I hung around out there awhile, then went back in and checked outside our classroom, just in case, and even in the resource center (talk about a long shot). There wasn't any sign of her.

In the end, I listened to some tapes myself and then drove

home. I told myself it didn't matter in the least, and what did I expect from some young kid like that? She could make it on her own through Spanish I. And if she couldn't . . . so?

Later on I told myself that this was like the isolated thunderstorm that comes and drenches all the hay right after you've just finished raking it and even have the tractor backed up to the baler. There wasn't any point in getting mad, or feeling sorry for yourself. Things happen; you accept them; eventually, you die.

I stayed up almost all night long that night, reading some and listening to music. I heard the "Steam It Open" tape a lot of times, of course; it always had the "Save her life" instruction in it. At maybe 3 A.M., I looked that situation squarely in the eye.

I was having an experience I didn't have a name for. Tara and my mother hadn't heard the words, so "Save her life" was *not* there on the tape, though I kept hearing it. It came from somewhere else, inside my head or out of it.

I'd gone to Sunday school and so I knew the stories in the Bible where the different prophets heard Jehovah speak to them. I subscribe to *Time*, and so I also know that even to this day, people do have visions.

Well, it seemed that I was having, like, a vision, but with only sound, no picture. I wasn't going to say that I was hearing *God* (a woman—kind of neat!), but neither was I going to rule that out. In any case, the message seemed benevolent, not evil. I totally accepted it.

And, in truth, I wondered if it might refer, somehow, to Mary.

6

THE NEXT DAY, Tuesday, we had Spanish class again, as usual. I got there early, also usual; Mary breezed in at the bell. She was in the row in front of me, and maybe five seats closer to the door. That day, the place smelled strongly of that special classroom disinfectant, the kind they use when somebody's thrown up.

For the entire period, my eyes stayed on Señora Markham or the Spanish book. I was aware of things I didn't look directly at, however. For example: Mary's head was often partway turned, in my direction. I accepted that but still ignored her.

She left the room before I did, and quickly. She had a blue-jean jacket on and khaki pants, and she was talking to another girl, Señorita Ringkamp. I felt relieved—and also disappointed, angry, and superior. Or possibly *inferior*.

But she was just outside the door, flattened back against the wall, when I came out. Then she was right beside me as I started down the hall.

"Oh, Shep, hi," she said, and she talked fast and ran the stuff she said together. "Sorry about yesterday but you see I had to babysit the neighbor's brat/I didn't know till Sunday night real late/My mother told her that I would without even asking me and so . . ." She took a breath. "Boy, didn't that room *stink*?"

It sounded like a speech she'd memorized, all except the last part. She wore a little smile as she recited it, a smile that flickered on her painted lips but never reached her eyes. It was as plain as day that she was lying through her overbite.

"How come you didn't call me up?" I said. "There's just the two Catletts in town, and both of us are in the book." It was better not to look at her.

"Call you up?" she said, and blinked. "Well, on Sunday, it was—would have been—too *late* to call. And Monday morning, well, I wasn't sure if you'd be up. I didn't want to call too *early*, wake up everyone, or anything, you know—"

I interrupted her. "I was wide awake in class that morning. You could have told me then, right after."

"Yes, but, well, right after class my girlfriend had to talk to me," she said, still talking fast, but not as fast. "You see, she had this *problem,* something really *personal,* you know? And real important."

"So, telling me you couldn't meet me *wasn't* so important?" I knew that I was acting like a jerk, but I couldn't seem to stop.

"No, no, *of course* it was," she said. "But it was just . . ."

And, suddenly, she stopped and grabbed my arm and made *me* stop and turn to face her. When I looked down, her eyes were very big, and slick with tears.

"Oh, Shep, I just *forgot,*" she said, her voice all trembly. "I'm really, *really* sorry. I remembered *Saturday* and *Sunday,* swear to God, but Monday, I don't know, and, well, the part about my girlfriend, that was true. And after school, I *did* go down with her to—I suppose I shouldn't say—but to the *clinic,* you know, and last night when I remembered,

39

well, I didn't *dare* to call you then. I hardly closed my eyes all night, from worrying. I'm really, really sorry, Shep!"

She did look sorry, too. There was no mistaking that. I began to think that with the weekend in between, it really wasn't too surprising that a person Mary's age, who wasn't all that *focused* (as I'd seen in Spanish class for close to six weeks now), would have an extra-study session slip her mind. And, I mean, I'm not exactly Christian Slater, after all. If you looked at it cold-bloodedly, you'd almost figure she'd forget.

"Hey, it's okay," I said. I almost didn't recognize my voice. "It's over." And I paused. I swear I felt a struggle going on between my ordinary self and this unruffled individual. This stranger.

"If you want to, we can meet some other time," I said. "I'd still be glad to try to help you. Here." I made a fist and tapped her on the shoulder with it. "Now we're even."

I almost couldn't believe how great that sounded, how mature and cool I suddenly was being. I'd made my point. I hadn't let her get away with anything, but neither had I been vindictive. And touching her, in the way I did, had made our whole relationship more . . . personal. This clearly wasn't any teacher-student thing.

"Oh, great," said Mary, smiling full intensity and taking a deep breath. "So, how about *today*? Same time, same channel? *Please*? I want to make it up to you!"

I wondered what she meant by that. Would her accent suddenly be pure Castilian? Or what? In any case, I felt my heart beat faster.

"I'll have to try to change some plans," I said. I didn't want to sound too eager. "Try to reorganize my schedule a bit. I'm not sure if I'll be able to." She had her lower lip between her teeth. "But I can try."

'Oh, *great!*" she said again. "I've got a class. I gotta run.

But, look, I'll be out there on the steps right after school. And I'll stay there for a half an hour, cross my heart." She made the cross; I watched her do it. "If you can't make it, well, I'll understand and . . . I'll deserve it!"

She started backing off, away from me, and skipping, crab-wise, down the hall. "But you'll really *try* to make it, right?" I nodded, adding on a little, easygoing smile. "Bye, *Shep!*" And she turned and ran, showing me her heels, in flat, black, ballet slipper sort of shoes.

I called my mom and told her something had come up at school. There was some extra work I had to do, I said. Would she tell Dad I couldn't make it to the barn, again?

Sure, she said at once. She'd also come and pick me up, just tell her when.

I said I didn't want her to do that. I wasn't sure exactly when I'd finish, but it wouldn't be that late, I said. I could hitchhike, catch a lift with someone going home from work, maybe even Tara's mom. *My* mom said she *really* wouldn't mind the drive; didn't I want to call her later and she'd just buzz down? I've already said that she was curious; she also was *persistent*.

Absolutely not, I said. I promised her I'd rather hitch. I swore to God. I was so sincere I almost wept.

She then admitted that was just as well. She'd promised Dad a pecan pie that night, and she had planned to can the applesauce—the *winter's* applesauce—that afternoon. This whole scene was typically my mom. Is it any wonder that I'm not a troublemaker? Can you imagine what a price I'd pay?

Of course I felt some pangs of guilt, as soon as I hung up the phone.

I convened with Tara right outside the cafeteria, and we went in to eat our lunch together. We almost always met for lunch on Tuesdays. We both brought sandwiches from home, and fruit. Sometimes I'd have some cake or cookies, too, but Tara'd spurn my offer of a half of all those idle calories.

"Get thee behind me, Catlett," she would say. "You little *snake*. Where I'm heading—Eden, Garden of—everybody's naked, don't forget. You wouldn't want them saying, 'Where'd *that* chubby cherub come from?' would you now?" Of course I'd shake my head, not only at her question, but also at the whole idea of Tara being viewed, *au naturel,* in Boston, by a hot-eyed, leering gang of Mitch-type strangers. Made me nearly break out in a sweat, that did.

Anyway, this Tuesday Tara munched her tuna fish and sprouts on whole wheat bread a little angrily. She told me she was going to take "the cockamamie SATs" on Saturday. I gaped. That was her sleep-in day, the morning in between her nights at Angela's. That also was (of course) the test you had to take to go to college. This was like an Amish person going for a driver's test.

"It's all your fault," she grumped, "for telling me that if I ever changed my mind, like *years* from now, I'd have to take the stupid thing when I was out of practice. It's been preying on my mind. You remember saying that?"

I didn't, but I nodded; it *was* the sort of thing I'd say.

"It's probably a total waste of time and money," she went on, "but Mr. Fryman said I ought to, too." Mr. Fryman was her guidance counselor. "The two of you are ruining my weekend; thanks a lot. I hate you, Shep. I really do."

I grinned. "Well, in that case, you'll be pleased to know," I said, "that I'll be staying after school this afternoon. The seat beside you on the bus will not be occupied by me. You won't have Shepherd Catlett there to kick around."

Tara had been staring at her sandwich, holding it in both

her hands. It was dripping on the Baggie it had traveled in. But now her eyes snapped up at me, below her heavy brows. She made them into slits. My Grand Inquisitor.

"How come?" Her voice dripped also, with suspicion. "How come you won't be on the bus?"

"I told you," I replied. "I'm staying here in school. I've got some extra stuff to do. Some Spanish stuff."

"*Spanish* stuff?" she said. "Again? Two days in a row, you've got some extra stuff to do for Spanish I? *Imposible!*" She said that with a Spanish spin: *Im-po-seeb-lay.* "I took Spanish I three years ago, remember? They haven't changed the teacher or the book, so Spanish I does not require any 'extra stuff' by you. Spanish I is not that hard, *amigo.*"

She glared at me. She was only being funny, kidding me, but still I felt defensive and accused.

"I'm helping someone out," I muttered, as I filled my mouth with meat loaf (ketchup, mayonnaise) on 'rye.

"Helping someone?" Tara seemed to think that over. Then she nodded; it was possible. "Like who?"

"You don't know her." I didn't look directly at the prosecutor. "Mary Sutherland, her name is."

And talk about coincidence, or chance, or *fate*—who is it that I see just then, way across the cafeteria, but Mary? She was sitting at a table with three boys, and wearing a white sweater with a big green *B* on it, crossed by a golden megaphone. It meant that she'd made cheerleader, rare for just a freshman. Cheerleaders at our school are special beings. All of them are pretty, and all of them are thought to be a little wild. People say they can "take care of themselves"; their faculty adviser can't—or doesn't bother to—control them. They all live in the Center and date jocks. That's what the grapevine has to say concerning cheerleaders; the grapevine's our main source of information, those of us who live on Highridge Road.

The guys with Mary Sutherland were not exactly jocks, however. So, what were they (you might ask)? *Trouble-makers?* Well, you *could* say that. One of them, named Gerry Mays, *had* been a jock but wasn't anymore, officially. He'd been a soccer player, the best one on the team, I'd heard, given to spectacular solo dashes down the field that ended with him firing the ball so hard that it could break the goalie's fingers. But the year before, he'd been caught with a six-pack on the team bus, and it wasn't the first time he'd broken team rules. They'd been coming back from playing Elman, I believe it was. The coach had kicked him off the team, his team, and this year Gerry'd said he thought he'd kick the coach off *his* team, turn and turn about. And so he never did go out for soccer.

He was a handsome, careless-looking guy, not serious at all. He often wore a leather jacket—brown, that aviator type—with chino pants and unlaced hundred-dollar sneakers.

Now he and Tipper Doane and Jeff McKee were playing keep-away with Mary's bag of chips, her little bag of Champs potato chips. They'd toss it back and forth and dangle it beyond her reach. Sometimes Gerry would hold on to *her*, just grab her so she couldn't reach across the table. He wasn't being careful about where he put his hands on her, I didn't think. But Mary only laughed and kept on trying to regain her lunch, that part of it. She didn't want to be a spoilsport, I supposed. I wondered how she knew those guys, all seniors.

Then Mr. Melchiorre come on over to their table. He's a Phys. Ed. teacher and a football coach, and he was pulling duty in the cafeteria that day. He was not the young, lean, smily, scientific sort of Phys. Ed. teacher, the kind I happened to prefer. He was more old-fashioned—in the worst sense of a word I like: an *animal*.

In fact, the animal he'd always made me think of was a bull; that was a little odd in that a lot of dairy farmers don't keep bulls these days. Our cows (to give you an example) are serviced by a Mr. Ralph Armbruster, who keeps some grade-A semen frozen in his truck and is, himself, a southpaw. But Dad remembers *Grampa's* bull real well, so I have heard a lot about the way the real thing looks and acts. Beauregard was heavy-built and powerful, with a big thick neck and a ferocious temper. He was also good and dumb. Mr. Melchiorre to a T.

When Mr. M. pulled duty in the cafeteria, he wanted there to be no "horseplay" whatsoever. I assumed that he was making, or remaking, that point clear to Gerry Mays and company. Gerry didn't look at him. He just took Mary's bag and squeezed it hard between both hands; the crispy contents must have been reduced to crumbs. Then he tossed the ravaged bag to Mary and stood up and walked away; the game was over. Mr. Melchiorre blinked, and shrugged, and then moved on, himself.

"Mary Sutherland?" said Tara. I turned toward her; she'd been watching me watch Mary. "She cute?"

"What? I don't know," I said. "I guess she sort of is." I tried to figure out how much to say. "She's just a kid. A freshman."

"A *freshman?*" Tara said. Her brows shot up; she flashed her sudden smile. "That's a dangerous age; you best be careful, Cats. Juliet was just a freshman, too, you know." She paused. "And look where seeing her got Romeo."

7

AFTER my last class, I waited for the crowd to thin out some, before I went outside. I saw her right away, sitting on the steps all by herself and way off to one side. She'd taken off the sweater with the big *B* on the front of it and just had on her blue-jean jacket once again. There was a bookpack on the step that she was sitting on. It leaned against her side; her elbows rested on her knees. Alone like that, and sitting there that way, she looked extremely young, and sort of . . . fragile.

I felt glad I'd given her another chance; I was doing something right by doing this. The last full bus was leaving the school grounds as I walked up to her. I felt more nervous than I thought I would. I welcomed "Save her life" into my mind. I was going to help her slay the dragon known as Spanish I. I, Sir Shepherd Catlett, Knight of the Round Silo, once and future member of some rural rescue squad.

It was another mild fall day. Mary asked if we could do this in the park, and I said fine. Burnside Center has some *stuff*—a lot of stuff—in it, for such a one-horse town. It has this park, for instance. Inside its borders are a public pool, a pair of softball fields, three tennis courts, a playground, and a bunch of picnic tables. There even are some modernistic sculptures scattered here and there, and made of metalwork, or granite. These all weigh tons and are unbreakable, of course. All of them are shaped and some of them are tilted, but none of them *resembles* anything.

Kids sit on these sculptures when they gather in the park. That day, regrettably, Gerry Mays was one such kid, and so was Jeff McKee, two other guys, and five or six assorted females—not that well assorted, come to think of it.

"Hi, Mair-*eee!*" somebody called as we passed by, a ways away. "Whacha *doin'*, huh?" I thought it was Max Edelman; his father was a shrink.

Of course I didn't turn my head. This had been a truly dumb idea, I thought. Doing it at all, for openers—*suggesting* it—and then coming to the park, *displaying* it. I wished that I'd gone home, been on the bus.

Mary also didn't look at them; she did, however, make a movement with one hand, in their direction. That produced some "Oohs," and what I took to be a feeble mooing sound. Pretty soon, there was the backstop of a softball field between the sculptures and ourselves. An empty bench appeared. We looked at each other, shrugged, and sat.

The Spanish went quite well, amazingly. Mary wasn't hopeless by a long shot. Her ear was pretty good, in fact. At first she was self-conscious and apologetic, but in time she got relaxed and concentrated on the words. I noticed that my tone of voice was like the one I'd used when talking to the captive fawn.

We kept on working for an hour. She wasn't used to studying, to *trying,* so I didn't want to overdo it.

"So, I saw you having lunch with Gerry Mays," I said, as we stood up to leave the park. Mr. Subtle, right?

I felt her eyes come up to check my face; Mr. Blank was looking off into the distance.

"Oh, yeah," she said. From the corner of my eye, I saw her shrug.

"Is he a real close friend of yours?" I couldn't help myself; I was thinking of his hands. "Him and Jeff and Tipper, Max—those guys?"

"No, not particularly," she said. "They're just some kids I know, from parties and that kind of thing. Gerry's dad lives down the street from us; *he* stays at his mom's house mostly, though." She laughed. "He says he's got the perfect mom. When she isn't out, she's out of it, he says."

We kept on walking. "I saw that you made cheerleader," I said. Gerry's mom did not seem like a subject worth pursuing.

"Oh, yeah," she said, a little more enthusiastically. "I really was surprised. I tried out, but only for the hell of it; I never thought they'd choose a freshman. I 'bout collapsed when I got told I'd made the squad. All the girls on it are really cool, you know? Like Amy Golden, she reminds me of that Laura Dern—the movie actress? I keep thinking she could be her younger *sister*."

I know who Laura Dern is. Tara's into movies ("film," she says); we have the VCR, she chooses. She thinks Laura Dern is "tough." I prefer the Julia Roberts type.

But thinking of the movies made me have a good idea: Why couldn't I take Mary to a *movie* sometime? On a Saturday, for instance, like this coming one?

I knew there was a foreign film in Dustin, a Brazilian one, I'm pretty sure it was. It'd be in Portuguese, I guessed—not Spanish, but the next thing to it. That'd mean the movie'd be connected to our work in school, which made it almost like a *field trip*, except it wouldn't be the whole class going. She wouldn't have to think about it as a *date,* unless she wanted to. And if she turned me down, it wouldn't necessarily be *me* she was rejecting. Lots of people can't stand reading subtitles.

Although I thought all that in less than fifty feet of walking, I still held my tongue. The trouble was, I couldn't seem to find the offhand, careless, almost *kidding* set of words to ask her with. So I decided that I'd call her on the phone instead. I'd even wait a day, I thought, until tomorrow night. That'd make me look less eager and more casual than if I asked her now, today.

What I wanted for the present time was that we'd part not just on friendly terms, but almost, well, as *buddies*. And so, when she began to thank me once again, I offered her a hand to shake. She left it out there, empty, for a heartbeat, but then came to and grabbed it—with her most enormous smile.

"If you ever feel the need to do this sort of thing again," I said, "you know where to find me." Mr. Funny.

"Hey, you bet. I learned a *lot* today," said Mary.

"Take it easy, then," I said, turning with a wave and moving off. I thought of that line from a commercial: *It doesn't get any better than this.*

And then it did.

"You're a sweetie, Shep," I'd swear she said.

Standing, waiting, with my thumb out in the road, I of course began to ponder what she'd meant by calling me a "sweetie." Was it a piece of fifteen-year-old shorthand, meaning, possibly, "a person who I like a *lot*"? Or was it just a light, low-level compliment, like when your mother says you've been "a real big help"? Or let's suppose that there's a third door: Could young Mary be a little tease?

49

An old tan pickup hit the brakes as it got close to me; it rattled off the road not far beyond. I'd recognized the driver and his chariot by then. Dwayne Delbert hadn't made the bus that morning, and he might have been in school or not; I didn't know. He hadn't been in Spanish class. But, luckily for me, Dwayne now was heading home. He had on a cowboy hat.

"D. Wayne. Thanks a lot." I clambered in. He used that time to get out cigarettes and fire up a Camel.

"Almost run right by you, Shep," he said. "Not many guys I know down here. Or not so's I'm about to pick 'em up."

"Well, I'm sure glad you spotted me," I said, and dropped my bookpack down amidst the cans and candy wrappers on the floor, between my feet. "I don't know 'fit's my deodorant or what, but I was starting to take root out there."

Dwayne laughed and nodded. I was comfortable with Dwayne, with how he was. Any time I talked with him, I let my SAT scores go, and dropped my *Time* subscription. I was much, much more like him than like that Gerry Mays.

"You down there at the school today?" I asked Dwayne now. Sometimes, if he didn't make the bus, he'd drive to school. But him not having Dwight with him suggested that he'd been to Burnside on some other errand.

"Nah," he said, and laughed again, and thumbed his hat back off his forehead. His hair was thinning in the front already, and his lower teeth were starting to change color. But his eyes, which were a very clear gray-blue, were what you noticed first about Dwayne. They made me want to call out something, the way you want to do when you walk in a cave. But Tara'd said to me one time that going only by his eyes and "facial bones," Dwayne was the best-looking boy in our entire school. I'm pretty sure she didn't mean that as a put-down; as you know, I've never claimed to be good-looking.

"You know what that damn school seems like to me, some-times?" said Dwayne. He spat out a tobacco crumb. I shook my head, of course. "Like one of them real *rotten* towns out west, back in the eighteen hundreds, or sometime. *You* know the kind I mean, where if a decent person rides in there, they have to take all *sortsa* crap." He laughed. "You see 'em all the time, on the TV."

I nodded, thinking of the mooing sounds I'd heard that day.

"And the teachers," Dwayne went on, "some of them are like the guy that owns the bank in Tombstone, or whatever. Guy that wears a suit and *runs* that town. Acts—or looks—respectable, but really is a rat? The kids in school, they're just 'the boys,' you know? Bunch of no-good sonsabitches, some of them. But that *banker* calls the shots." He took a deep, deep drag and blew out smoke. And then he laughed again.

It didn't take much time to make it out of Burnside Center and begin to climb toward Highridge Road. The road that we were on, called Coffin's Hill, once had some dairy farms along it, too, my dad had said, but now the pastures and the cornfields had grown back to trees and brush. Most of the houses that were now on Coffin's Hill were newer, off the road, sited at the ends of curving hardpack driveways. Their owners wanted "privacy," and so the road itself still had a country look to it, with all that second growth along the sides. Even in the wintertime, you hardly got to see those "gentle-men's estates" at all.

"You doin' any good with coon huntin'?" I asked. The

season had begun the Saturday before. Hunting seemed a better subject, as compared to school.

"Not *too* bad," Dwayne replied. "And may do even better." He pointed at the glove compartment. "Take a gander."

I opened up, and right inside there lay a Ruger .22-caliber single-six revolver, stainless steel with a white grip, holstered on a coal-black gun belt. You could see the outfit wasn't new, but it had been well taken care of, treated right. The leather had the pleasant smell of saddle soap on it.

First, of course, I whistled, then said, "May I?" with a head bob toward the gun. I never pick up someone else's firearm before I get permission.

"Sure," he said, and so I took the whole deal out and laid it on my lap. Then I pulled the pistol from the holster and gave the cylinder a spin to see if it was loaded; it was not.

I'm no hotshot with a handgun, and so I haven't handled tons of them, but this one of D. Wayne's felt good to me: how it fit my hand, the balance that it had. You don't need a big old gun to knock a coon down from a tree. Assuming that you want to, in the first place, which I don't.

"Real nice," I said, and meant it, in a way. Ruger makes a real fine gun.

"Mmm," said Dwayne. "Can't wait to get back home and pull it once or twice. We've got them buscalero holsters, home."

"Ho," I said. "You gettin' into quick-draw, Dwayne?"

And he said, "Some. A little. Me'n Dwight, we practice now and then. They got that contest at the Midville Fair, y'know. I wouldn't mind to go in that, someday." He laughed. "Yeah, I could see me doin' that." He flicked his Camel out the window.

I shook my head the way we do on Highridge Road, the

way that means "Hey-o, imagine *that*," instead of "No," and then I slid the holstered gun and belt back in the glove compartment. I, too, could see Dwayne doing that, drawing-down real fast, his gray eyes flat and empty underneath his hat brim.

I wouldn't want to be behind the target if he did, I'll tell you that much.

8

"*WELL,*" Tara said to me. We were heading homeward on the bus on Wednesday afternoon. "I know who Mary Sutherland is *now*." She paused. "*My, my.*"

I didn't have to turn my head to know what she was looking like. Not a Celtic princess, but a tarty little brat. Although I'd never say I *liked* that look, I also wouldn't say it made me genuinely mad. I'd often feel a bit like *spanking* her, perhaps—but that's an altogether different trip, I guess. As a rule, I keep a reasonable, defensive calm.

"'My, my'?" I said. "So, what's *that* meant to mean?"

"Oh, nothing," Tara said. She did a little head-toss. "Or—just that, yes, she sure *is* cute. Especially to those of us who like our cuteness on the babydollish side."

"*Baby*dollish?" I repeated. "I'm not sure I follow. I said she was a freshman, didn't I?"

"This doesn't have to do with age. Not necessarily." Tara shook her hair around again. It wasn't only thick and black, it also glistened, wickedly. It was the sort of hair a guy might like to stroke, and bury both his hands in. "Babydollish is a kind of . . . attitude. Think of a personality made up of ribbons, lace, and ruffles, and which wears the cutest little panties in the world. But which also is completely see-through." Tara chuckled.

"Hey, time out!" I said. I held my left hand up and placed the other palm on top of it. "Yesterday you didn't know a thing about the girl, and now you're . . ." I groped for some way to express my indignation. "Well, you're driving the *manure-spreader* over her. I *swear*." And *I* shook *my* head, looking down.

"Don't act so serious," she said. "Where's your sense of humor, anyway? All I'm giving you is one small slice of girls' room gossip, modified—*enriched*—by my effective use of simile and metaphor. As preached by Mrs. Keenan in your English class, if you'd just pay attention."

I peeked at her. "What was it that you heard, exactly?" Then I shrugged. "I'm mildly curious." I cleared my throat. "She didn't seem like all that bad a kid, to me."

"We-ell," said Tara. It was definitely annoying now, how much she seemed to be enjoying this. "Actually, the story seems to be that Mary's got her mom believing she's completely sweet and innocent. *She* thinks she's always at the *library*, or doing volunteer work at the Senior Center. Or baby-sitting for some people who don't have a telephone. But what she *really* does is hang out with that Gerry Mays and all his scudzo friends. I hear she's always at their parties, and she's more or less their little . . . *mascot*." Tara gave that word a nasty spin. "That's how she got to be a cheerleader, they say. Everybody knows about it but her mother, so I understand."

And myself, I thought. That information hadn't been in *Time*, and so, as usual, I wasn't in the loop.

I stretched both legs and raised both arms and tried to manage a convincing yawn.

"*I* don t know all that," I said. "And none of it has anything to do with Spanish, which, as you know, is the—*piedra*, is it?

rock?—on which our whole relationship is built. The only one. And, as a matter of fact," I added, still offhandedly, "it's possible I'll help her out again." It had gotten to the point that I could hear the "Save her life" voice in my head at any time I wanted to. Like then, right then. "Turns out she's pretty smart—just a little scatterbrained." I wrapped a grunt around a little laugh, and promptly overdid it. "We were all that way at her age, I imagine."

"Oh, *absolutely. Sure,*" said Tara. "Why, back there in the ninth grade, it was all that anyone could do to get you to do *any* schoolwork, Shep. You were such an absentminded, happy-go-lucky, out-of-focus little airhead, weren't you?" She grunted, too—disgustedly. "Tell me about it, bubba. You were conscientious from Day One. At five minutes old, you probably helped clean up the delivery room." She switched into a little-baby voice: "Sah-wee I bwot all dis mess awong wif me. . . ."

I deserved that, I suppose. Doing my *hermano grande* (yes, big brother) bit, I'd gone too far.

"Oh, by the way," she said. "*I* need Shep to help me, too. It's a favor he *swore* he'd gladly do, if I got stuck sometime. And now I'm stuck." She looked at me, her lower lip between her teeth. "But it's a biggie."

"What?" I said. "What is it?" I was on my guard.

"Saturday night," she said. She made a yikes-type, guilty face. "I need a ride. A ride back home from work. Mom only let me know today—she's taking off for Hartford, visiting her sister Clara. Thanks a lot, Mom. I'd thought I had the car, but now I don't."

My lips pushed out into a pout; it was as if my whole "accepting" side had skipped the neighborhood. And left a sulky baby in its place. There would be no Brazilian movie for *hermano grande* and the fair Maria. There simply wasn t any time for doing that *and* picking Tara up at Angela's.

"No Mitch?" I said. Not gracefully. Mitch had often picked her up on Saturdays, I knew. And brought her home. Eventually.

"No," she said. "If you *must* know—no, no Mitch. Not that Mitch, or no-Mitch is . . . the point, exactly. When I tell you that I need a ride, it seems to me that you, a college-bound high-school senior and a National Merit semifinalist, would probably assume—*deduce*—at least one other fact: that no one *else* is giving me a ride. Not Mitch, not Fitch, not Sam and Dave, not Crosby, Stills, or Nash, not Young; not Manny, Moe, or Jack, not—"

"All right, already," I broke in to say. "I get the point. I shouldn't have said anything. All I meant was—"

"Yeah, yeah, yeah," she said. There was a thickness in her voice I wasn't used to hearing. "I know exactly what you meant. And look, if you don't want to pick me up—or just remembered that you have to study Spanish verbs that night with someone—you can say so. I'm sure that I can figure out some other way—"

"No, no." I interrupted her again, this time with a smile. I laid an ambassadorial hand on her forearm. Tara was my oldest friend; we weren't into being mean to each other. I squeezed her arm. I always liked the way she felt; she had real muscles. I thought (for possibly the hundredth time) it was too bad the two of us were so alike. "Opposites attract," the saying goes, and Tara, clearly, was attracted by a different sort of guy. *I* was attracted by young Mary Sutherland. I *could* have been attracted by ol' Tara Graza, if *she* had been attracted by me.

"I'd like to pick you up. I really would," I said. And it was true. Even when her feet and back hurt, and she didn't think a hundred-dollar tip would make her smile, she was my neighbor and my friend. "I'll be there at what time? Ten-thirty?"

"Eleven might be better," Tara said. Her voice was back to normal, but she didn't look at me. She was picking at a loose thread on her jacket's sleeve. "Then, I'm pretty sure you wouldn't have to sit around outside." She sighed. "I know it's a major favor, Shep. I'm asking you to, basically, give up a weekend night. You promise me you don't have something else you want to do?" The tarty little brat was back to being . . . oh, the gracious queen of Highridge Road.

"I promise you," I said. And weirdly and amazingly, I meant it. I'd wanted to ask Mary to a movie. I still would get around to doing that sometime. But helping Tara was a thing that Shepherd Catlett simply *did*. A habit he'd picked up, somewhere.

"Mitch and I," said Tara in a real soft voice, "have not been getting on too well. It's probably my fault. But I only see him after work, when I'm worn out and feeling pretty bitchy, as a rule." She shook her head. "And it seems to me he's starting to act different, too. More like he's doing me a favor. Giving me a break by seeing me, when he's so busy, busy, busy."

I shook my head, too, and made some sympathetic clucking sounds. Inside, those clucks were tra-la-las. I'd never met, or even seen, this Mitch, but my imaginings were less than stellar. I'd decided he was sandy-haired, and balding, and wore glasses. And had very clean, well-manicured white hands—and peculiar furniture and art in his apartment, and a lisp. He definitely was not the man for Tara.

"I'm sorry," I said, insincerely—dishonestly, I guess. "But I guess it's best to find that sort of stuff out now."

"Instead of when?" she said, a little sharply. "After we get married, do you mean?" She laughed; no, make that *sneered.* "Get real, Cats, will you? These Mitches I go out with aren't anyone I'd ever think of getting serious about. I'm *seventeen,* for God's sake. I'm not about to trade the trap I'm in for . . . well, an even bigger one."

"Mmm," I said to her, agreeing, and relieved, and trying not to grin. I, still seventeen myself, was apt to look at every girl I saw (*did* look at every girl I saw) in terms of: Would I want to marry her? After a decent interval, I opened up my Physics book and started whistling.

When I pulled in the parking lot in back of Angela's that Saturday, twenty minutes earlier than Tara'd asked me to, there still were customers inside. I could see that, through the windows, and their cars were lounging here and there around the lot.

But that was perfectly all right with me. I was not in any rush, and Tara wouldn't have to wait when she was done. Whenever she looked out the kitchen door, she'd see her chariot awaiting her.

One reason I was not in any rush was that I had a lot to think about while waiting there. Something had happened earlier that day that had . . . excited me a little. Or maybe not *excited;* maybe I should just say *interested.* But that's an understatement, really. The right word *is* excited.

While I was eating lunch, the phone had rung. My mom answered it, as usual. But it was for me—not usual.

"Yes, just a moment, he's right here. May I ask who's calling, please?" my mom said. Of course, I thought it was for Dad.

Then Mom said, "Mary Sutherland," holding the receiver

out to me. She did that altogether casually, as if it were a commonplace event. As if she did it many times a day, sometimes saying, "Drew Barrymore," sometimes "Michelle Pfeiffer."

My father was sitting there beside me at the kitchen table, pretending he hadn't even heard the phone ring, pretending he was deaf and spoke no English. He was feigning total interest in the paper that he'd propped against the iced-tea pitcher. But his lips were also moving as he stared at it. Dad was being funny.

"Hello," I said into the phone, expecting I'd hear Tara's voice.

"Hello—Shep?" she said. And it was Mary. "I hope I'm not disturbing you or anything. But I was wondering. . . . You doing anything on Tuesday night?"

"Tuesday?" I began. I tried to think. I'd be doing homework, naturally. What else did anybody do on Tuesday nights?

"No, nothing in particular," I said.

"Well, how'd you like to come on over here—to my house—after school? Or wait a minute. Not *exactly* after school, but after cheerleading practice. I guess, around, oh—five o'clock? And maybe we could—*you* know—do some Spanish, and after that my mom would give us dinner. And after *that*"—she giggled—"we could watch TV or something, till you had to go."

"Sure," I said. My mouth was dry. I tried to lick my lips, and I could feel my father being careful not to look at me. My mother had put dishes in the sink and turned the water on, not hard. "What time should I come over? Five? Five-thirty? Something like that?"

"Yeah, five," she said. "Is this a bad connection? I gotta

jump in the shower, after I get home. We really get all sweated up at practice usually." I heard a voice say something in the background, on her end. "Oh, right. Excuse me, Shep. I shouldn't have said 'sweated.' " And she laughed again.

"Mmm," I said. I was having trouble finding things to say. "So, okay, then. I'll see you five o'clock, on Tuesday." I was ready to hang up.

"Okay . . . but wait, Shep. Don't hang up. You don't know my address, do you?"

"Oh, no," I said. I don't know why, but I was blushing. "Better give it to me." And I touched the pocket of my shirt.

My mother, turning from the sink, picked up a pen that had been on the windowsill in front of her. She set it down by my place at the kitchen table, and with it a piece of paper from the yellow pad she used to make up shopping lists.

"One-fourteen Cedar," Mary said. "You know where that is, don't you? Cedar? And we're the fourth house on the right."

"*Got* it," I said, energetically. I didn't need to write it down, not with that memory of mine. Cedar couldn't be that hard to find; it'd be near Pine or Maple. One-fourteen, the fourth house on the right. My mother waited, looking at the pen and paper.

"Thanks now, Mary. Bye," I said, and carried the receiver to the phone and hung it up.

When I turned from doing that, Mom and Dad were looking at me, both of them.

"Mary?" said my mother.

"Sutherland," said Dad.

"Kid that's in my Spanish class at school," I said, looking at the microwave. "I'm helping her with her pronunciation. She wants me to have dinner at her house, on Tuesday."

"Mary Sutherland?" my father asked.

"In your Spanish *I* class?" said my mom.

"Adios, amigos," I replied to both of them, and left the room. I didn't feel like having parent-child relationships just then.

Since hanging up that phone, I'd had all sorts of thoughts—but always coming back to "Save her life" and "You're a sweetie, Shep." This relationship was clearly taking on . . . momentum. Mary had asked for help again, more help. She also wanted me to meet her mom, or maybe mostly vice versa. Mrs. Sutherland would see the kind of person that I was, a senior boy who'd helped her daughter with her homework, and who wasn't . . . Gerry Mays. If Mary said she wanted to go out with me—say, in another week or two— Mrs. S. would surely say okay.

I didn't think at all about that babydollish business, other than to totally reject it.

I must have closed my eyes for just a moment, imagining myself walking into Mary's house and meeting Mrs. Sutherland and saying, "Hi—I'm Shep and I've been sent to save your daughter's life," and so, before I knew that she was out of Angela's, Tara was beside me in the car.

"Hey," I said, and checked my watch. "Five minutes early, even."

"Thank God for any favors," she replied. "Even tiny fractions of an hour. And thank *you*, too, for being early, Shep. Five minutes more in there, I might have gone at someone with a salad fork."

"That bad," I said.

"Incredible," she answered.

"Customers or management or both?" I asked.

"Both," she said. She'd put her seat belt on, and then had slumped down in the seat, her chin down near her chest. "But mostly customers. They're such a bunch of hypocrites and . . . *weasels*. Probably their sons'll be up there at the University with you. Four-wheel-driving all across the lawns and knocking up some high-school girls because a condom 'spoils it' for them. And saying that they certainly *assume* a chick'd use protection, if she's gonna 'ask for it' like that."

"Gee," I said. "I can hardly wait to meet my roommate."

She sat up a little, turned her head to look at me.

"I wonder how they work it," she began. Without looking, I could tell that she was smiling. Tara's moods went back and forth when she was really tired. "D'you suppose they'll match you up with somebody like you, another hayseed? Or would they try to put you with some totally outrageous rich kid from New York? So that the two of you would cancel each other out?"

"You could make those questions moot, you know," I said. "All you'd have to do is change your mind and come to college with me. We could live off campus, maybe." I knew I hadn't quite achieved the tone of voice I'd wanted. I almost didn't know what I was saying; stuff had just popped out.

"What?" said Tara. "*Huh?* What's going on? *We—would live—together?* Did Mom put little mushrooms in your supper dish tonight, by any chance?"

"Look," I said. Suddenly, I was annoyed. And tired. But my mouth ran on and on. "All kidding aside. Do you want to know what I *really* think about college, and about you, and about *me* and you, and about—"

I have no idea what might have followed. Something. If

she'd said yes, I would have told her some damn thing. And I'm pretty sure it would have been the truth. I was prepared to reach for it. I *think* I was.

But—"No." She cut me off and sat up straight, and now she wasn't smiling, and she wasn't kidding, either. "I'm much too tired and disgusted and upset to hear . . . *anything.* Except . . . except, oh, nonsense. And the radio."

She reached out and flipped it on, and hit a Dylan song.

Dylan said it wasn't *him* some "babe" was looking for. But neither of us laughed.

9

ONE-FOURTEEN Cedar, the fourth house on the right, was not the least bit babydollish. I don't think *anyone* would say it was. It had these two big spruces on the little lawn in front of it, so you could barely notice that it was brick and plain. With not a ribbon, or a ruffle, on it anywhere.

I rang the bell and waited. It took a while, but finally Mary's mother came and opened the front door.

"You must be *Shep*," she said, and put her hand out. "We're *so* glad you could come."

I shook with her. Her hand was thin and dry. The rest of her was slender, too. She had on a denim skirt that buttoned down the front, a light blue work shirt, and a multicolored silk bandanna knotted Western-style around her neck. She wore her dark brown hair in bangs and parted in the middle; it was straight and didn't reach her shoulders. Her nose and eyes were a lot like Mary's, but her lips were thin, and there were lines that ran down to their corners from the edges of her nose. The smile she used to welcome me kept flicking on and off.

"Mary's still upstairs," she told me. "But I'm sure she'll be right down." She turned her head toward the staircase. "Mary?" she called out. "*Shep's* here, sweetheart!"

There wasn't any answer from above. The stairs were heavily carpeted; the house felt solid, almost soundproofed.

I followed Mrs. Sutherland into the sitting room. There was a small brick fireplace with black wrought-iron tools beside it, a couple of high-backed rockers, and a couch and matching easy chair, both with flowered slipcovers. A grandfather clock in the corner said that it was three past five. The tables all had books or other things on them, such as a hurricane lamp, a piece of pottery, a stack of woven coasters, a brass candlestick. On the walls there was a nice round mirror, a couple of little shelves supporting plates on little racks, and some prints of cozy-looking country scenes. Unlike our sitting room at home, this one did not contain a TV or a stereo. And on the mantelpiece there was a saucer that had something burning in it, giving off an unfamiliar smell.

"Don't mind the 'stink,' as Mary calls it," said her mother. "Actually, it's Chinese herbs. They have a *host* of therapeutic properties. But I know she wouldn't want me to get started on all *that*." She took a big deep breath, with her hands clasped tight, chest high. "How about a glass of cider, Shep?"

"Fine," I said.

"Well, *good*," she said, and flashed that quick, uncertain smile again. "I'll fetch. And you just roost in here. Be comfy."

I chose a rocking chair, and roosted. It was completely quiet in the house, except for the ticking of the clock. I laid the hand that held my Spanish book on my right thigh. Nothing happened, so I crossed my legs and opened up the book, and started to reread today's *Lectura*.

Footsteps suddenly came bounding down the stairs, and there was Mary, looking breathless. She was wearing blue long pants that looked like sweatpants, that material, but much, much tighter. And big red, poofy bedroom slippers, and a red-and-blue-striped turtleneck, an oversize. Her hair was still a little damp, but she had pulled it back and tied it with a bright red ribbon. She looked really, really *clean*.

"Hi, Shep! Sorry to be—hey! Oh, *bitchin'*, Mom . . ." she started. Waving one hand back and forth in front of her face, Mary veered away from me and went to jerk the window open. Cold air blasted in. When she turned from it and back in my direction, it was clear she wasn't wearing anything above the waist, beside that turtleneck.

"Well, here we *all* are finally," said Mrs. Sutherland, re-entering the room and holding a thick and squatty little glass, full almost to its dark blue rim with apple cider. She handed it to me.

"Fresh-pressed," she said, "from Davidson's. Their apples all are alar-free, you know. That's the one place you can trust their produce with your life." She laughed. "Which is exactly what one does, of course."

"Thanks," I said, and quickly took a sip before I spilled it. The cider tasted fine to me, about the same as any apple cider.

"But Mommy, you trust Catlett Dairies' *milk*, too, don't you?" Mary said. "I told Shep you always buy it."

"Yes, indeed I do," said Mrs. S. "I think it's perfectly delicious. Fresh, whole milk, unprocessed, just as Mother Nature made it. And of course I trust it. You know," she said to me, "Mary's like a farmer's daughter, if only in that one respect. All her life, she's had whole milk to drink. And look at her! I ask you—isn't she a perfect dairy-poster girl?"

I didn't have to look. Mary would have been a great advertisement for our product.

"Yup," I said, and nodded hard. My ears felt hot. "Oh, absolutely." Mary'd moved around behind her mom, and now she opened up her mouth and stuck two fingers deep inside it.

"Well, I know you've got some *work* to do, you two," said Mrs. Sutherland. "So I'm just going to take a hike and let you get right at it. Hope that you like free-range chicken, Shep. And that you brought your appetite!"

"I guess I do, and yes, I did," I said. I wasn't sure what "free-range" chicken was. The range we have at home is an electric.

"See you later, Mom," said Mary, as her mother headed off.

But moments later, she was back again. She had a sleeveless gray wool sweater in her hand this time.

"I think you'd better slip this on, dear," she announced to Mary.

Mary'd accidentally left her Spanish book at school, so we sat together on the sofa and shared mine. She moved as close to me as she could get, saying that she really needed glasses but hated how they looked on her, and didn't know how anyone could stand to put "those contact thingies" in their eyes. From the outsides of our knees up to our hip bones, we were tight against each other. At one point, as a little test, I moved my leg an inch or two away. But hers came after it at once. It hadn't been an accident; she wanted us to be in contact and together, close as grease on home fries.

(Looking back, I'd say it was right then, while we were doing Spanish, that I proposed this thesis to myself: Mary was changing, and she needed—*wanted*—an alternative to the kind of boy she had been seeing, to the Gerry Mays–type guys. At first, she'd probably been flattered to have older boys'—and girls'—attention. She would've liked the limelight, getting to be much the youngest cheerleader. But then she probably had started hearing what some other kids were saying, like that "babydollish" business. How could she escape the trap she'd gotten into? What better way than by acquiring a very different kind of boyfriend? The voice that told me "Save her life" was just another force or factor, pushing in the same direction. It wasn't only Mary and myself who felt that it was time for us to have, and work on, a relationship.)

When Mary's mother popped back in to ask if "five minutes would be *good* for dinner," Mary didn't move away from me. In fact, and to the contrary, she sort of dropped her head down on my shoulder.

"That'd be just *super*, Mom," she said. "Shep must be really *famished*. He's been working like a *Trojan*, helping me."

After Mrs. Sutherland had gone back to the kitchen, though, she turned to me and, looking mischievous *and* puzzled, said, "I've never understood that: 'working like a Trojan.' Unless it just means working *good*, the way a Trojan better had." She laughed and winked at me. "D'you think that's it? Not going all to pieces on the job?"

She shook her head and then kept going.

"Can you believe my mother used to use some kind of *sponge* for birth control? She thinks the Pill is dangerous to your health. It and fluoride toothpaste, which she says can give you cancer. If you use it as a *spermicide*, I guess it could." She laughed again.

"Yeah," I said, and gave a little laugh myself. And then, looking at my hands, "Could I just use your bathroom?"

"Sure," she said, and told me how to get to it.

I found that I was nodding by the time I washed my hands.

I'd been surprised, but basically I loved her lack of inhibitions. The phrase that came to mind was this: Beyond my wildest dreams.

Dinner was all right. We sat around three sides of a square table, off the kitchen. Mrs. S. had cooked the chicken in a red clay pot, and there was rice, and lots of salad, and some seedless grapes and bananas mixed up with yogurt and honey for dessert. Mary's mom did not have any chicken; instead, she had a little bowl of beans and seaweed, which she mixed in with her rice.

"Mom's a total veggie," Mary told me, cheerfully. But when she saw that her mother wasn't looking, she made tight circles with one finger, right beside her ear.

She also told her mother lots of things about yours truly, some of which I didn't know she knew. For instance, my being a National Merit semifinalist. Of course, that had been mentioned—well, announced—at school, but most kids didn't know or care what it was all about, and managed to forget the news as quickly as they heard it.

"I'm hoping *Mary* will go on to college, to the University," her mother said. "In today's world, everybody needs an education and a résumé. No one can count on anything, or any*one*. Years and years ago, a girl could look ahead to marriage, children, and a home. People didn't *get* divorced, or nowhere near as frequently. Men were more responsible. They made commitments that they planned to *keep*."

"My father is a rock and roll musician," Mary said.

Of course that sent *my* eyebrows up.

"Among *many* other things," her mother said, before I had a chance to ask what band or bands he'd played with. "We've been divorced for fourteen years," she said to me. "I'm afraid he was, and is, a very immature, unfocused individual."

I believe I nodded, staring at my plate and thinking that I might have used that word, *unfocused,* to myself, describing Mary. But she, of course, had every right to be a little immature. She was still a kid.

"What Mommy *means,*" said Mary slowly, "is that Daddy is a fall-down drunk."

"*Mary!*" Her mother kind of gasped the word. "I'm sure that Shep did not come here to learn that kind of thing." She turned her fleeting smile on me. "Luckily for us, that's ancient history, as far as we're concerned. I prefer to think about the present moment—and the future. About more *interesting* subjects. *Is* the family farm endangered, do you think? One reads these stories in the paper, and they had a piece in *Time.* . . ."

Of course I had to give her our reaction—Dad's and mine—to both the local situation and the larger issues they'd brought up in *Time.* While I was talking, Mary dropped her hand on top of mine. It—my hand—had just been lying on my place mat, on the edge of it, when she did that. She took me by surprise. We never had held hands before. I saw her mother's eyes shift slightly when it happened.

After we had finished our dessert, I helped to clear the table, over Mary's mother's protests. They had a dishwasher, and Mary said that she and I would load it up. Her mother told her she should not be silly, *she* would do it, but it wasn't any use. Mary pushed her mother out the kitchen door. I washed the pot the rice had cooked in, and the salad bowl, while Mary put the dishes in the washer.

"My mom can turn this on before she goes to bed," she said to me, "after she's finished with her herbal tea." She made a face and then said, "Here. Let me."

I'd started rolling down my shirtsleeves, standing by the sink, but she came over after saying that and relieved me of the job. The last time anyone had buttoned up my shirt-sleeves for me, I was four or five, I'll bet, and "anyone" was Mom. Their techniques were pretty much the same, except I don't believe the tip of Mother's tongue was showing.

"We could go up to my room and watch a little tube, or listen to some music," Mary said. "Unless you have to rush back home, that is."

Mary's room was nothing like the way that *Tara* probably imagined it. There weren't teddy bears all over. It was very neat, with hardly any . . . personal effects in view. Unlike Tara's room, for instance, it didn't give you any clues about her tastes, or friends, or . . . anything.

There was a big TV, however, aimed directly at the bed. Mary flipped it on, then took her sweater off and flopped down on her back, her head up on her pillow. The TV dial was set for MTV. I pulled a maple chair around so I was sort of sitting next to her. It was just a single bed, and she was lying in about the middle of it. I considered asking her about her father, but decided that might be unwise.

"You were really nice to do this, Shep," said Mary. The sound of anything we said was covered by Sinead O'Connor. "Sorry about Mom. She's about enough to drive . . . the *Pope* to drink."

"Oh, she's not that bad," I said. Me playing the good Shepherd, right? "I thought she seemed real smart. And that chicken tasted great."

"Well, she was blown away by you," said Mary. "I could tell. You got me lots of brownie points. She's after me to read the papers, all the time. It pays to be informed, she's always telling me."

I smiled and nodded noncommittally. "I thought you laid

it on a little thick. All that about my—*you* know—academic stuff."

"Yeah, but—well, at least I didn't tell her *other* things," said Mary, and she wrinkled up her nose at me.

"Like what?" I said.

"Like, oh, how much I like your bod," said Mary. And for the first time, all night long, she flashed that really major smile of hers. "How I'd been turned on by your looks before I even noticed you were good at *Spanish*."

"Oh, yeah, sure," I said.

"You think I'm kidding?" Mary said. She looked down at her chest, made a bit of a production of it. "*I* may tell some fibs sometimes, but *them,* they never lie."

Of course I'd looked when she did, *where* she did. And yes, her breasts had made their point, I guess you'd say.

"Mmm," I said. "I'm flattered."

(You may find that totally pathetic, my reply. But I was improvising, don't forget, trying to sound as if I didn't find these goings-on at all unusual. As if I was a guy whose road of life was often lined with . . . what? *Erectile tissue?*)

"And I sure like the way that *you* look, too," I added. "Lots. In fact, before you spoke to me that day, I'd been trying to figure out if there was any point in asking you to go somewhere with me, sometime. Starting with a movie maybe, or whatever. No big deal."

I was treading daintily, I hoped, but treading. I didn't want to push too hard, but I also didn't want to miss an opportunity. I mean, she *had* been kind of coming on to me all night. It didn't take *Burt Reynolds,* say, to notice that.

"I'd like to do that, Shep, and more. I really would," she said. "Sometime. The trouble is, right now I'm sort of breaking up with someone. An' he—this boy—is kind of weird, an'... *sensitive*? I mean, I can't just say, 'That's it; screw you,' and walk—you know? He might crack up completely. Or get *violent*. He's got a really crazy streak like that; his friends have told me things he's done. It's just that kind of situation. I bet you've had to do the same thing with a girlfriend, maybe. Handle someone with silk gloves? Try to let them down real easy?"

I nodded, at a loss for words. Oh, sure; "silk gloves" were standard dress on Highridge Road. The trouble was, though, given what she'd said, I really didn't have a choice.

(The other trouble was: I felt a small suspicion suddenly take root inside me. I wondered if I might be being used. She'd mentioned getting "brownie points," and tried to make it look as if ol' Shepherd was her boyfriend. Plus, or once again, I still—regrettably—remembered all that garbage Tara'd told me.)

I don't know how I looked, while I was thinking that. What I *do* know is that Mary, after watching me a moment, said, "Oh, Shep," and slid right off the bed and sat down on my lap, with both her arms around my neck.

"All this is really *hard* for me," she said before she kissed me. On the lips and with her mouth soon softening and widening until it was a *cavern*, with a devil-tongue inside that darted wetly here and there, exploring, making lovely kinds of trouble.

I'd put my arms around her, too, and had my hands spread on her ribs when I began to feel a tugging under them. Mary was pulling on her turtleneck, yes, pulling *up*. I naturally permitted that. Material slid underneath my palms, and soon my hands were on her hot, smooth skin. And then—aha!—she gave a wiggle with her body, turning it so that my right hand, under cover, moved onto her small left breast.

Don't misunderstand. I'm sure—well, *pretty* sure—that

I'd have made that happen on my own, given a little time. I won't say I'd never touched a girl that way before; I had. But this was the first time someone had *demanded* that I do so, more or less. Someone who seemed to care for me, that naturally, that much.

She moved a little, not to get away, however. In fact, she got my right wrist in one hand, making sure that *my* hand stayed exactly where it was; every time my fingers touched her nipple, she would make a little moan or whimper-sound.

But then I felt her other hand go searching on the fly front of my pants. Searching, yes, and *finding*. Her mouth escaped from mine just long enough to say, "Oh, Shep. Oh, *wonderful!*" Her fingernails were trying to figure out my belt when, through the music, dully, we both heard her mother call.

"Mary? Telephone! The phone's for you, sweetheart!"

Then getting closer, "Mary! Can you hear me, honey? It's for you!" That was followed, shortly, by a knocking on the door.

Mary scissored off my lap, reclaimed her sweater, got it on, checked her hair while passing by the mirror, and pulled back the door.

"Sorry, Mom," she said. "I guess we had the music on too loud."

While she was getting up, I'd grabbed the Spanish book from off the floor and opened it, and laid it facedown on my lap. I couldn't think of getting up, no matter what good manners specified.

"Wait right there a sec," said Mary. "Before you go, I need for you to show me something else." Her eyes were sparkling, that yard-long smile was back in place; she was having *fun!* "The . . . whachacallit, conjugation of *venir*. Wait'll I get off the phone, okay? I'll just be half a minute."

She went charging down the stairs. Her mother smiled at me and hesitated, then went after her.

In fact, I got downstairs before she came back up. That had been much, *much* too close a call. I needed to regroup. I also had a lot of homework still undone. Although perhaps I would regret this judgment—this decision—later, I decided that the verb "to come" would have to take a raincheck.

She was hanging up the phone as I went in the living room.

"I really ought to head on home," I said to her. I looked around. Her mother wasn't in the room. "If you could thank your mom for me . . ."

Mary walked me to my car, out front; I held her hand in transit. When I had my seat belt on, she popped her head inside the window, and we kissed. That proved to me the first one wasn't just a fluke; she was one amazing kisser.

"Thanks for understanding, Shep," she said to me. "Thanks for *everything*."

I wanted to say something meaningful and future-oriented. Nothing worthwhile came to mind, so I settled for a simple, understated truth.

"I'm really glad I came," I said, and turned the key.

She answered something with her eyebrows up, and laughing; it got lost in engine sound. She waved; I pulled away and made a U-turn, headed back down Cedar Street. It seemed as if I was a different person than I'd been when I turned up it.

Before I'd gone a half a mile, I found that I was missing her.

10

A ND SO there then began, for me, a time of life I wasn't quite prepared for. And, right at first, I didn't (couldn't) just accept it—me, the farmer's son, the very one who claimed he'd learned to be so placid, hanging out with cows and Mother Nature. No, for a period of days, I turned into a less-than-honest, music-loving, *Time*-subscribing, horny little *jerk*.

I imagine everyone goes through a period like this, at some point in his life—a time when there is something/ someone that he wants a lot, and just can't have. I imagine there are those (and wouldn't it be just my luck to be one?) who go through lots of periods like this. Whose lives are just one hunger followed by another. "You can't always get what you want," insists another classic by the Stones. Imagine if, instead of "always," you got "ever"!

They started in on me the first thing Wednesday morning.

"So," said Mr. Subtle, a.k.a. my dad, at breakfast. "How was Mary Sutherland?" When I'd come in the night before, the thumbscrews and the rack had been (to my amazement) out of service, and the members of the Inquisition on their break, apparently. I'd made it to my room without a single question being asked of me.

"Fine, thanks," I now replied. "She's almost over her malaria. Kind of you to ask." I put on water for poached eggs. Poaching eggs requires one to move around a bit. I wasn't going to be a sitting duck for them.

My father saw that he was up against a transient wall of stone. But farmers are resourceful. He backed up and tried to swing around one side of it.

"That's wonderful," he said. "So, probably the two of you were able to have fun unlimited, doing stuff like counting up to ten in Spanish, and spinning one another's verb wheel. Did she cook dinner, or did you?"

I walked right into that one, saying, "What? Cook *dinner*? Neither of us did. Her mother cooked for us."

"Oh, was *she* there?" asked my father. "She didn't head on out?"

"No, of course not," I replied, oblivious, with quicksand up around my waist.

"Ah," said Dad. "I must've made a false assumption. You weren't *baby-sitting*, then." He cackled, totally delighted with himself.

"Very funny, Dad," I said. My poaching water boiled and got turned down. I gave it one quick stir and broke the eggs into it, fast, before the spinning stopped; that way, they held together better. I could sense my mother watching me. She'd taught me this technique, of course. I felt as if I'd just appeared on Stupid Pet Tricks.

"What *did* you have for dinner?" she now asked. "Anything that *I* might want to make sometime? Something new and different, and delicious?"

"No, not really, Mom," I said. "Chicken, rice, and salad. Mary's mother isn't in your league. She's actually a vegetarian."

"Oh?" my mother said. "But Mary *isn't*."

My mom, as you've just seen, is much, much slicker than my dad. She'd managed to extract one fact concerning Mary Sutherland from me. The stone wall had been breached.

"No," I said, recovering, "she eats the same as we do. One leg at a time."

My mother smiled. She could afford to.

"And *Mr.* Sutherland?" my father said, and coughed. "*Kaf-kaf*. What does *he* do, may I ask?" He was doing comedy again, pretending to be Father, from the age of Queen Victoria.

"Oh, he's with Procol Harum," I informed him, fingers crossed.

His eyes betrayed him. I could see he didn't know that Procol Harum was a major rock band, years ago.

"That'd be those lawyers over there in Dustin," he threw out, wild-guessing. I could hear that *tinge* of doubt, uncertainty.

"There's just no fooling *you*, big guy," I told him, spooning out my eggs, remembering (so much too late) I hadn't started toast.

"Oh, by the way," said Mom, "Tara called last night. I told her you were out at Mary Sutherland's. She said there wasn't any message." She paused. "I hope that was all right, my saying where you were." She said that in her Ooh-I-didn't-make-a-booboo-did-I? tone of voice. The one I'd always found completely lacking in sincerity.

"That was perfect, Mom," I said. "Just perfect."

Let her figure that one out.

Tara dropped into the seat beside me on the bus, as usual.

"*Boy*," I said to her at once, "am I exhausted! Went to

Mary Sutherland's to eat last night, and didn't get back home till half past nine. That's when I started working on the little writing sample Keenan wanted us to do. I think mine probably is even *leaner* than she had in mind. How long is yours?"

My strategy was simple: Volunteer the information she may think you're trying to keep from her. Act real casual and not at all defensive. Ask a lot of questions. Tell yourself you're someone else, Joe Cocker for example, and get by.

"So, now the rock on which this whole relationship is built is not the Spanish language *only*," Tara said. "Now, there is *food* involved as well. *Arroz con pollo,* probably."

Luckily for me, our Spanish class had not yet gotten into menus, so I didn't know the meaning of *arroz con pollo,* which is chicken and rice, or "rice with chicken," properly. It would have freaked me out to have to think that maybe Tara had Seen All, Knew Everything.

She, meanwhile, was looking like a troublemaker. She was also looking . . . good. Underneath the open CB jacket she had on, she wore a V-necked top that buttoned down the front and then tucked in her pants. It was made of what I think is known as "fleece," and it was tight. Her breasts were much more of an event than Mary's, and for a moment I imagined—wondered—how they'd feel, if I had one or both my hands slid underneath her top. Good, I thought. Tara would feel good all over.

"Joke if you must," I said, "but I am really helping Mary. She hasn't had an easy life, you know. Her folks split up when she was just a baby. It sounds as if her dad might be an alcoholic, and her mom's a vegetarian."

Tara looked over at me strangely. "Gee," she said, pouring on the irony, "that's tough. I can't *imagine* what that must be like for her."

Of course I felt like dirt the second she said that—like

scabs, like pesticide. How I'd forgotten, for the moment, that *she'd* never had a father either, growing up, and that she hated living with her whiny mom, I'll never know. Except I did know. My mind was totally preoccupied with breasts and Mary. My famous memory had gone off on a holiday.

"I didn't mean she has it all *that* hard," I babbled. "It's just . . . my parents have been giving me the third degree. Because I go to someone's house for dinner doesn't mean it's like some big *romance,* or anything. . . ."

Tara turned again to look at me when I said that, and kept on looking this time. I was staring at my hands, doing a careful study of a thumbnail picking at a cuticle. When she spoke again, she sounded altogether different.

"No, it doesn't *have to* mean that, not at all," she said. Her voice had lost its edge and gotten soft and rounded, gentle, confidential. "But . . . well, *does* it?"

I had to answer that, of course. She'd asked a simple question; it was up to me to give a simple, honest answer. I thought it even might feel good to tell someone, and talk the whole thing out, the ambiguities and all. *"Hey, that's what friends are for"* went running through my mind. I didn't have a better friend than Tara. Or any other friend at all who I'd *confide* in.

"No," I said. *"Of course* not. *Jesus!"* I did a bunch of head-shakes, one hand now a fist and rapping on the windowsill. "She's just a kid I'm trying to do a favor for. Like you were saying, she hangs out with certain people. . . . I thought if I could get her to—*you* know—get good at something *regular,* in school. . . . It's probably completely crazy. . . ."

Tara didn't look away. I could tell that, even though I didn't look at her. And I could also feel her take a hold of my near hand and squeeze it.

My heart sank. How *could* she?

"That's typical of you," she said, in that same measured, sweetheart tone of voice. "You are the *nicest* guy, I swear. It's tough to be a girl her age, growing up not knowing any men, except for teachers and the kids at school. I was lucky, spending so much time around your dad and you. I didn't get attracted by the outlaws. And in my case I suppose I've always known"—she laughed—"I *could* be good at school-work."

"God, *yes!*" I put my other hand on top of hers and squeezed it back. I was feeling terrible; I would have liked to *cry* and rend my clothing, beat my breast. I'd lied to Tara, flat-out lied, and she had not just *bought* the lie, she'd over-paid me for it.

"You're the smartest kid in our entire *class*," I said to her, in a burst of absolute sincerity and painful neediness. I needed, desperately, to make it up to her. To give her even bigger compliments than she had laid on me was a begin-ning. I had to start another streak of honesty: tell the truth about a hundred times, real fast, to try to cancel out, or cover up, that one big lie.

"Not to mention the most *gorgeous*," I went on. "By a country mile," I said.

Tara pulled her hand away from mine and gave my nearest wrist a little slap.

"Hey, down boy! Let's not lose our foothold on reality, all right?" she said. "You have a reputation to uphold, you know."

In the state that I was in, those words confused me. Reputation? Me? For what? For not hitting on the girls? For never giving her a compliment?

"For honesty," she finished.

Groan. I started to protest. The huge humongous lie I'd

told her wasn't even close to being canceled out. I almost felt like going back and telling her the truth about my thing (whatever it was called) with Mary. Almost.

"I don't believe you *or* my mother," Tara started up again. "Not when you start in with that 'gorgeous' crap. You're both required to say stuff like that. But speaking of that little writing sample . . ."

I let the conversation go, but I kept sneaking looks at her, all the way to school. She would hate me if she ever learned the truth about that lie. *Gorgeous* really was the word for her. And I'm not only talking about body stuff, believe me.

It was *Mary* I was hot for, though; it was Mary who was hot for *me*. But it was Mary, too, I couldn't have—or even take to Dustin, to the movies. Not until she finished kissing off this other boyfriend that she had, the unknown soldier. Other groan.

At least I got to see her every day in Spanish class. For someone else, that might have made it worse, but not for me. Well, maybe not for me. I'd look at her, and I'd remember. My memory for certain things was still intact. Visual and tactile memory, I had. And, after class, there was the opportunity to talk to her a little, in the hall. A very, very little.

The first two days, our conversation just pertained to Spanish. I didn't want somebody overhearing us and saying anything to you-know-who. Or *Mary* didn't want, to be completely accurate. Her work had started to improve. She got a 90 on the quiz we took the day after our dinner; Señora Markham looked a little unprepared for that. On the third day I was moved to mumble, "How's the disengagement going, anyway?"

She shook her head and said, "Not awful well." She

sighed. "He's started counseling, an'—*I* don't know—it seems as if I oughta not give him a lotta grief, just while he gets that going." She shook her head again, and said, "It's real confusing, Shep. You *know* I'd like to be with you, but . . . uh-oh." Señorita Ringkamp was approaching.

"So, *ad-e-os* now, Señor Catlett," Mary said to me, loudly and dismissively. *"Muchas gracias por los . . . notas?* Notes? I'll give 'em back to you *mañana."*

And giving me a wave, she cruised off with her friend.

The next day, during class, she turned around and winked, and made a little kissy mouth at me. Memories came flooding in, et cetera. I swear.

The weekend gave me kind of like a welcome recess, in a way. I couldn't look to see who Mary might be having lunch with; I didn't have to hang around the halls in hopes of watching her pass by with just some girlfriends.

I faced the fact that doing all that spying stuff fed into my suspicions, at the same time activating any tendencies I have to see myself as what I really am, I guess: unlikely, as the object of a girl's desire. *Was* there any Mary's violent boyfriend? (I would wonder, or re-wonder). *Was* I merely being used? Or was it possible her kisses (and the rest) were every bit as honest as . . . as . . . as my uncle Elbie thought I was?

I didn't know, and that was why I'd hung around the halls and cafeteria, when I was able to. Half the time I seemed to see her with a guy, or guys—though never any one enough to make me sure that that was *him,* her (former?) one and only. Yes, I mostly suffered in the hallways.

So, Monday, back at school, I made a resolution. I was going to change my attitude and . . . habits. When I had free time, instead of hanging out, I'd spend it studying, the way I used to. Until it got too cold, I'd even go outside the school and sit up in an empty grandstand by one of the athletic fields. I'd long ago discovered grandstands were the perfect place to get some reading done. Nobody disturbed you; there was never anyone but me in grandstands in the morning. I'd get back to grandstand-reading, I decided, Monday, during second period. No more theorizing, analyzing, thinking foolish thoughts.

Well, you'll never guess what happened.

I got out there, sure enough—weather cool and cloudy. I climbed up to the top row of the grandstand nearest to the gym. I opened up H. Melville's masterwork, and heard the sound of . . . high-pitched voices. When I looked up, I saw a girls' Phys. Ed. class, streaming out onto the field in front of me. They all wore shorts, and some of them were kicking soccer balls. Almost at once, a game began. And sure, the best one on the team with white tops on was Mary.

Melville, H. could not compete with this—not with Mary in the flesh. I'd known her legs were long, but seeing them when they were mostly bare from midthigh down was still a revelation. Now, it made good sense to me they'd want her leading cheers, a girl with her coordination and physique. She was really good at soccer. Instead of chasing frantically around the field, the way a lot of players did, she'd cruise in one direction and the ball would seem to come to meet her. And then she'd dribble it a ways, or pass it artfully ahead, or sometimes shoot, and score. I smiled to watch her do all that, and stuffed her every graceful move into my waiting memory.

I decided, then and there, I wouldn't try to fight them, the very basic feelings that I had. There wasn't any point in worrying: Was Mary doing this or that? *Was* there any other boyfriend?

I'd been chosen, I decided.

Fate had plucked me from the pool of all young men throughout the universe (or anyway, the town of Burnside), and made me fall in love with Mary Sutherland. *Fate* had put me in the Spanish class with her, so that I'd learn her wants and needs; *Fate* had brought me here, today, to see her once again.

Today had deep significance, I thought. Even when I *tried* to get away from her, I couldn't.

Does all this sound (at least a bit) familiar?

I was back in my "accepting" mode, again.

11

THE NEXT DAY, I was back there in my grandstand seat, the same time as the day before, my Melville in my hand.

I didn't know if Mary'd have Phys. Ed. again, or if she did, if they'd play soccer. I didn't have to know. If she did . . . well, fine; I would appreciate her every move, her lovely lineaments. If she didn't, also fine; that was equally acceptable. Reading Melville would provide a different kind of . . . fun.

What I was doing (I explained to me) was being sure I was . . . *available*. I wasn't hiding from her, on the one hand, or searching for her (on the other). Whatever Fate decided . . . that would happen.

I waited. Nothing happened. I sighed and opened up my *Moby Dick*. Today would be the opposite of yesterday: Fate had decided I would study. Did the sigh I'd sighed denote some disappointment? I wouldn't want to say, but if it did . . . well, I accepted that.

The grandstand I was sitting on was not a solid concrete structure, like the one they have on one side of the Alumni Memorial Football Field. This one was made of wide gray wooden planks, supported by a metal framework, maybe twenty rows of them in all. So, sitting on it I could see what was behind me, just as well as I could see the field in front. Behind the grandstand was the new wing of the high school, the one that had the gym in it. And partway through that period, I heard a gym door open. Naturally, I turned around; after all, it possibly was Mary and her friends. Maybe fate had issued them new gym clothes, even shorter shorts, and so delayed the start of soccer.

Well, it wasn't them. It was, however, someone else I knew, Dwayne Delbert. He was halfway dressed for Phys. Ed. class, in that he wore a bright red sleeveless shirt—the kind they made you wear if you were on the "Red team" on that day—and a pair of hightop sneakers. But he also had on jeans, instead of the shorts or sweatpants they wanted you to wear. But when he got outside, he pulled his Camels out and lit one. Then, he leaned back up against the building's wall and crossed his feet, and just relaxed and smoked. That wasn't in accordance with the rules, but D. Wayne looked content.

For perhaps a minute and a half, the only living things in that vicinity were Dwayne and me and three crows walking on the soccer field. But then the metal door that Dwayne had used real quietly came open with a bang, and out came Mr. Melchiorre. That's right, the bull-like Phys. Ed. guy and (so it now appeared) Dwayne's teacher for that period.

Mr. Melchiorre has a little group of favorites. They call him "Coach," or sometimes "Sarge," and halfway do his job for him, handing out equipment, taking roll, and spying on the other kids. They can get away with anything. The rest are treated more like prisoners on punishment detail. The smartest thing to be in Mr. Melchiorre's class is inconspicuous.

Dwayne, apparently, had tried to take that to the max. By

sliding out that door, he'd made himself invisible. But probably some kid had told on him, one of Mr. Melchiorre's suckbutts. So, now the Phys. Ed. teacher and his sometime student, D. Wayne D., were facing each other, there behind the gym, with no one else (they thought) around to witness what transpired.

It started out like no big deal. Dwayne kept his cool and held his pose, leaning back against the wall, that Camel in a corner of his mouth. Mr. Melchiorre faced him, spoke. I recognized the tone of voice, but couldn't make out words. Dwayne laughed and answered at much lower volume; I barely saw his lips move.

The next thing that I knew, Mr. Melchiorre had him by the throat. In his other hand, he had the cigarette he'd snatched from D. Wayne's lips. He held it with the lit end pointing out, away from him, and aiming it. It looked for all the world as if he planned to snuff it out on Dwayne, possibly in one of his blue eyes.

Dwayne's reaction was pure Highridge Road—to not put up with that. To try to kick the teacher in the kneecap.

He didn't make a real good job of it, however. In the first place, they had started out too close together. Dwayne couldn't see what he was aiming at when Mr. Melchiorre had him by the throat like that. And, too, he only had on sneakers, which are fine for jumping up and down, and running, but aren't worth a damn for kicking someone.

But what his trying did was set that Mr. Melchiorre off.

"Kick *me*, willya?" the Phys. Ed. teacher bawled. And then he called Dwayne something that you aren't even going to hear out in the barn, even with a Holstein tromping on a dairy farmer's foot.

At the same time, he leaned into Dwayne and, having

dropped the cigarette, hit him in the gut with what was certainly the hardest right-hand punch I'd ever seen, not counting on TV.

Dwayne looked as if he'd broken in half. Mr. Melchiorre moved a little to one side; his doubled-over victim started to go down. But Mr. Melchiorre wasn't done with him. While Dwayne was falling, he stepped in and hit him three or four more real good shots, right in the back—like, left-right-left below his ribs, and then one final right that landed where his neck became the middle of his shoulders.

Dwayne lay there on the ground, not moving. Mr. Melchiorre went back in the gym, but not before he'd got some more things off his chest. Standing over Dwayne, his heavy legs splayed wide apart, he shook his finger at him, in the way that people do when they are warning other people. I think I might have heard the word *assault* in there.

By the time I'd clambered down the grandstand steps, once the coast was clear, D. Wayne was sitting up and leaning back against the wall. His eyes were squinched up, closed, and both his arms were wrapped around his middle. He was hurting awful bad; you didn't have to be some Mitch-type guy to be aware of that.

"D. Wayne," I said to him, when I got close. "It's Shep. Are you all right? I saw what happened here, the whole god-damned routine. I was right up in the grandstand. I'm going to take this to the principal. He isn't going to get away with this. Are you *okay*?"

Dwayne cracked his eyes the second that he heard my voice, and then he winced and groaned.

"The hell he can't," he also said. "He owns this town, like I was telling you the other day. He'll say that it was . . . what the hell you call it? *Self-defense.* The mizzububble *bastard.*"

He rocked in place a little, testing, and he made another wincing sound. And Dwayne is country, don't forget; this is one tough kid.

"Do me a favor, will you, Shep?" he said. "Help me over to my truck, all right? I'm not that bad. And then go in and tell my brother Dwight to get my stuff that's in my locker. I ain't crawling back in there today, I guarantee you that much. No way, no how. I wouldn't give that suh-m-a-goddammed *bitch* the satisfaction."

Of course I did the things he asked me to. I still wanted to report the stuff I'd seen, get that Melchiorre kicked out on his ass from school, maybe put in jail. It hadn't been a case of self-defense. It was a teacher beating on a kid because he wanted to.

But Dwayne, he made me promise that I wouldn't say a word to anyone. He said this didn't have to do with me, or with the principal. It was between the two of them, him and Mr. Melchiorre. He said he'd work it out. He insisted he could drive okay and even winked at me before he started up, and smiled a ghastly smile.

That night, I telephoned his house and got his brother Dwight. Dwight said that Dwayne was fine, just fine, and that he'd gone out hunting coon, and so I couldn't talk to him, right then. I pretended I believed him. We don't push ourselves at people, up on Highridge Road.

12

I DIDN'T TELL my mom or dad about D. Wayne and Mr. Melchiorre. I was afraid they'd go "adult" on me, and have to be completely . . . *fair*.

You know the feeling I'm referring to? I bet you do. There are certain situations maybe no adult can fully understand— when *fairness,* for the moment, is beside the point. My parents never would *condone* what Mr. Melchirre did. They definitely would not approve of anybody, ever, beating on a kid. But they'd also almost surely feel obliged to point out Dwayne's "poor judgment." That (after all) he shouldn't have cut out of gym, or smoked, or answered back, or tried to kick a teacher.

I didn't want to hear that, so I called up Tara. I knew that she could keep a secret and I had to tell *somebody;* hey, suppose I dropped dead overnight? Also, and right then, I craved the sound of someone else's outrage. Getting mad at something with another person always makes me feel a little better.

Tara was the perfect other person; she didn't even let me finish.

"That *thug,*" she seethed. "That great . . . excretion! He's got no right to be a teacher, Shep. He shouldn't be; he *mustn't* be. Who do we go to, though—the Board of Education? Or the principal? How about your buddy Mrs. Vail, and the entire PTA?"

"Well, there's just one little problem," I said. I told her what I'd promised Dwayne.

"Hmm," she said. "That *is* a problem." I was sure that she was wrapping hair around a finger. "But—you know what I think? I think it's possible that other people might have seen what you did. Or that Melchiorre'd *tell* somebody. I wouldn't put it past that big fat slob—to brag about the way he showed some stumpjumper. One way or another, everything that happens in that school gets out, you know *that's* true. I'll bet you, pretty soon there'll start to be some rumors. And once there are, I think that Reese'll check them out. He prides himself on knowing everything." Mr. Reese was principal of Burnside High, and not too bad a guy, in fact.

We only talked a little longer after that. Just long enough to say how much we liked D. Wayne, and to air some other reasons that we had for hating Mr. Melchiorre. There wasn't any shortage of material. Toward the end, we got around to things such as the style and texture of his hair, the way he parked his car, and how he sometimes tucked his shirt inside his undershorts, in back.

It only took till after Spanish class, the next day, for me to find that Tara knew her Burnside High, all right. The rumor mill was going strong; other people knew, had heard, about the incident, at least a *version* of the incident. My source was Mary Sutherland, right after I had exited the classroom.

"Hey, Shep," she bubbled. "D'you hear what happened to . . . I think his name is *Wayne*, the one that's in this class? Except he doesn't come that often? He wasn't here today.

You know the one I mean? D'you hear what happened to him? This is really *hot*."

Me, I kept my cool.

"No," I said. "What happened?"

"Well, apparently this Wayne guy went whachacallit—puh-*serk*? Is that the way you say it?—and attacked this Phys. Ed. teacher, Mr. Melchioni," Mary said. Her eyes were huge. "They say he had a *knife*. But Melchioni kicked the shit out of him. Just with his bare hands." And Mary giggled—though not at her absurd non sequitur, I didn't think.

"It's *Dwayne*, not Wayne," I said, a little grouchily. This wasn't quite the rumor that I'd hoped for. "Do people actually believe that story? I mean, the part about the knife?"

"Sure," she said. "*I* do. Don't you? Did you ever see his *teeth*? That Dwayne's? They say that Melchioni had his back turned, and Dwayne went after him and tried to stab him. Right behind the gym. But what he didn't know, I guess, was old Melchioni used to be in the *Marines*, or something. An' so he'd taken, like, a *course* in what to do. Even with a knife, Dwayne didn't have a snowball's chance." She shook her head.

"Well, I know Dwayne," I said. "He'd never try to stab a teacher. I wouldn't go believing everything I hear—or spreading it around. Whose story is this, anyway?"

Mary looked confused; my reactions were all wrong, I guess.

"I don't know." She tried a smile. "I heard it from some kid, who got it from a friend, I think. I'm not completely sure."

I decided to be stern.

"Well, your story's all screwed up," I said. "Believe it. Dwayne's just as good a kid as . . . anyone. If any teacher beat on him, I hope that Mr. Reese'll find out when and where and why and damn well throw the book at him. Dwayne *never* tried to stab a teacher, I can guarantee you that. And people shouldn't say he did."

Mary bit her lower lip.

"I didn't mean *I* thought he did," she said. "I just thought you'd want to hear the story, Shep. I'm just telling you what different ones are saying. Don't be mad at *me*."

I looked at her as she was saying that, and naturally, my anger went away, to be replaced by . . . lust, wrapped up in tenderness. Mary was my love and my excitement. Her reaction to this D. Wayne–Melchiorre rumor was a normal kid's reaction. It was overly accepting, neither thoughtful nor mature, but—what should I expect from her? She'd learn better over time. Wasn't that where *I* came in?

Now, still looking worried, Mary checked the hall in both directions and stepped forward, getting close to me.

"There's something else I wanted to, like, *ask* you, Shep," she said. She was speaking softly; she was also speaking fast. "It's on another subject. D'you think you could, uh, maybe show me where you live sometime—your farm and all? Like, take me for a ride up there some afternoon? I bet it's really beautiful. You know—the country. Even with the colors gone."

"Sure," I said at once. There'd be some complications, but so what? This was a way that we could safely get together. I was ashamed I hadn't thought of it myself. How did that saying go? "Out of the mouths of babes and sucklings . . ."? *Right*.

"Maybe tomorrow would be good," I said. Now we'd see where Fate stood on the subject. "Assuming that you're serious." I tried to give old Fate a nudge.

"I am," said Mary, speaking softly still. "Tomorrow would be great. I've really missed you, Shep."

I nodded, and she turned away and hurried down the hall, top speed. Me, I sauntered in the same direction, senior-style. Getting Melchiorre canned was still important, on my mind, but hell, I also had my life to lead.

The plan for the next day that I came up with wasn't quite as simple and . . . straightforward as I would have liked, but that was more because of how my parents were than anything. If they had been a little more mature—*considerate*—in their approach to my relationships, I would have done things differently.

But, failing that, there had to be a "story." Luckily for me, such a story came to mind quite easily.

I could tell my mom I had to have her car to go to Dustin for some early Christmas shopping. That would explain the many miles I'd have to put on it, in case she looked at the odometer. (It also was *almost* the truth, in that I *wanted* to do early shopping, and I *would* next week, with Tara, in *her* mother's car. I was pretty sure she'd go for that. I'd end up doing just exactly what I'd *told* my mom, except a few days later.)

My only other small concern was making sure my parents wouldn't see the car (or me, or us) at any time that afternoon. The answer was that Mary'd have to see things at a little distance—our house and barns, the neighborhood. I'd give her *views*, which would *include* our place. *Everyone* loves views; ask any realtor. The little roads that ran off Highridge Road were famous for their views; ask many high-school kids. Couples drove from Burnside to admire them, most every weekend night. I could nose our Buick off the road, I realized, and we could then get out and walk a little ways, and see some sights that ought to take her breath away.

We'd be sort of *like* a couple, doing that, I thought.

13

I PICKED UP Mary at the public library in town, a half an hour after school let out. That was her choice of rendezvous. I didn't see a sign of her out front, and so I pulled into the parking lot behind the building. But when I started to get out, to go and look for her, she suddenly was there, beside the car, as if she'd sprung out of the ground.

"Perfect timing!" she exclaimed, as she got in. She waved a book at me. She then bent over, trying to fit the book into her bookpack. That turned out to be a major undertaking. Or at least she made it into one. A certain kind of person would have thought she was avoiding being seen with me. (Not that he really blamed her.)

She finally came up for air just as we reached the edge of town. We were about to pass the mall where Tara's mother works—but no, the red light caught us. So, guess who walks across the road, right then and there? Here's a bunch of clues: It was someone who I'd driven down to school that morning. And told that I was going to the dentist after school. Someone who I'd just *assumed* had gone home on the bus. Yes, Tara, in the flesh.

I think she saw us in installments. First, she recognized the car, my mom's old Buick. And so, of course, her hand came up to wave. Then, second, she saw me, and so the wave matured and added on a grin. But finally, in the third place, she saw Mary. Then she looked not mad, or glad, but, well, *embarrassed*. The hand came down, the grin removed itself, her eyes went quickly mall-ward.

"Is she a friend of yours?" asked Mary, as we started up again. "I think I've seen her in the hall, at school. Haven't I? She's really pretty, don't you think?"

I nodded, mumbled something back. I felt chilled. Tara'd caught me in a lie—two lies, counting what I'd said to her concerning Mary and myself. I had a sense of having squandered something valuable, something I might never have again.

Mary kept on babbling away—about the girls in school she thought were pretty, and how it seemed to her the only really handsome boys were in the senior class. She shifted in her seat and got a foot up under her, then put a hand out on my shoulder, started playing with my hair. At that point, Tara left my mind. I started thinking that I wished the Buick had a bench seat in the front. I'd always liked the way it looked when there's a girl way over on a bench seat, by the driver—in a pickup, say—when all there is, inside, is just the two of them.

The first thing Mary noticed, up on Highridge Road, was that a lot of folks have satellite dishes by their houses.

"I hear that they bring in a hundred channels," she said. "Cool."

But moments later: "Doesn't it get *lonely*, though, sometimes? This far away from everything? Like me, my mother'd have to drive me everywhere." She made a face. "I'd really, really hate it, if I couldn't just get up and *go*. If *she* knew every place I went.

"I thought there'd be more cows," she said, a little after

that, and then she asked me could I milk a cow. I told her that we used machines, but yes, I did know how to milk by hand.

"Is it really hard to do?" she asked. "You kind of pull their tits, right? But is there, like, a *trick* to it?"

"Not a trick," I said. "It's more of a technique. You have to practice for a while, before you get it down."

"I'll bet you're good at it," she said. "I'm *sure* you are." She laughed and touched my arm. "I *know* you have great hands."

Tingling inside, I turned the Buick onto what is now named Burnt Hill Road. People used to call it "the road to the dump," before the town dump got shut down. It's a narrow gravel road that only has six houses on it, none of them year-round.

"Isn't your place on the *main* road, Shep?" she asked.

"Oh, sure," I said. "But, well, I'm going to show you it from up above. You'll get to see our house and barns, and the entire acreage. And miles and miles beyond." I smiled. "In other words, a view, a real fantastic view. We'll only have to walk a little ways, I promise you."

With that, I nosed the Buick off the road and started to get out.

"Hey, hold on there, buddy," Mary said.

She grabbed my arm and pulled me toward her. I'd been looking forward to exactly what she had in mind. Mary was a freshman, but if she ever took a kissing SAT, she'd score up in the 1400s.

We kissed a real nice while.

"Ever since you picked me up, I've wanted to do that," she finally said.

"Me, too," said Uncle Elbie's nephew. And then he said,

"Come on. You've gotta see this view." I suppose that that was typical of me.

"O-*kay*," said Mary, but for a moment then she didn't move. Her head was turned toward me, resting on the seat back, and she smiled a little smile.

At last, she said, "You didn't bring a blanket, did you?"

A blanket? No, I'd never even thought of that. I popped my forehead with a palm. "Damn!" I said. "Forgot."

She nodded, smiling still. She seemed amused. "That's okay," she finally said, as she got out. "We've got a beautiful backseat."

We walked up to the high point of the former-pasture-gone-to-brush that I had parked beside. Someday, someone's going to put a house up there, my dad has said for years—and then tell all his flatland friends he's got a view "that takes your breath away." But even Dad admits it is a beauty. It goes on for miles and miles, way up the valley, with the mountains purple in the distance.

But the short view's also pretty fine. Looking right straight down from where we were, you see our place—the house and sheds and barns—and Highridge Road, and down on into all the nearby valley land, almost to the edge of Burnside Center.

I think our place looks even better from up there than from the road in front of it. Our house is big and rambly, white, with tall black shutters, two brick chimneys, and some nicely pitched slate roofs. It looks real solid—safe and homey. There are flower beds and bushes next to it, and the connected woodshed, at this time of year, is full of split, stacked firewood. My father's father was a stone-wall guy, and so there is a beauty all along the front, a ways off Highridge Road.

Mary was impressed.

"Boy," she said, "this is really *neat*. Your house looks *huge*—I guess it is. How many of you are there? Kids, I mean." I pointed at my chest. "You're an only child? I don't believe it!"

We spent perhaps ten minutes, standing there. I made sure she saw our swimming pond, and where I'd built a treehouse in the orchard. I pointed out the not-too-distant hill where I was pretty sure I'd seen a catamount the year before. Just as we were leaving, Mary said she thought she'd like to have a place like that someday, "When I'm a whole lot older."

Then she grinned at me and said, "Right now, I'd settle for a van."

When we reached the Buick, she got in the back. I followed closely after, then got cool and hopped in front to turn the heater on. At least she didn't have to tell me. Mary took her jacket off; she had on a chamois cloth shirt underneath. *Just* a chamois cloth shirt, it turned out.

I didn't have specific goals—*a* specific goal, *you* know—in mind, when I got in the car. Guys often do, I guess. In general, I wanted to repeat the kind of fun we'd had before, together. I wasn't carrying—or *owning*—any birth control, and that meant there were limits. And the girl was just a *freshman,* after all.

It didn't take us long to get to more or less the place where we'd left off at her house. That was wonderful; touching her like that put me in heaven. Then Mary took her mouth away from mine and said, "Let's just . . ." With one hand, she pushed up my T-shirt and my sweatshirt, with the other one she unbuttoned her tan chamois cloth. The message couldn't have been clearer. I pulled my stuff off, overhead. As I did that, she slipped out of hers. That made things even better. I kissed some brand-new places, where she wanted to be kissed.

Soon, and not surprisingly, I felt bold fingers on my belt. This time I was ready, and I helped her. Being ... well, a normal guy, I guess I'd hoped that she might want to do this—sometime, yes, today. And I'd decided that I'd let her. Freshman or no freshman, she seemed to know what she was up to; I didn't think I'd be ... corrupting her at all. This wasn't something I'd had done to me a lot of times (or, well, *before*), but it was something that I wanted lots, right then.

I started trying to reciprocate, but Mary muttered, "No. No, no. I have my period. This is good, like this; just kiss me, Shep." I did, and it *was* good—incredible, the best, I soared. And I'm sure a portion of my pleasure came from ... well, her audible delight, the way she *rooted for* the things that happened. I'd never done stuff with a *cheerleader* before.

We started back toward Burnside Center, with Mary chatting up a storm. She sounded wired and delighted. After a while, she started telling me that she'd been doing homework lately—not only for her Spanish class.

"I'm doing really *good*," she said. "It's neat. And it's all thanks to you. I've gotten to be—"

"*Intimate*," I said.

And she said, "What?" And giggled.

"Intimate," I said again. "We're intimate, that's why. It's just the greatest feeling. Me, I never realized what it meant before."

"Really?" Mary said. "Tell *me*."

"It means much more than 'close,' " I said. "It's like we've crawled inside each other's skin."

"Oh, Shep," she said. "That's weird."

"No, it isn't," I went on. "It's great. It means we think a lot the same. There isn't any obstacle between us. I can tell you anything, and vice versa. There's nothing we can't do with one another."

I could see her nodding, from the corner of my eye.

"I like your saying that," she said. "It's so *romantic*." She was quiet for a moment. "You sound real happy, Shep."

"I am," I said. "I think I'm happier than ever in my life, before. I'm telling you the truth. I've never been in love before, but I'm in love with you. I know it."

It was amazing, hearing me say that. It seemed so totally *adult,* to be in love with someone.

"Wow," she said. "In *love.*" There was a longer pause this time. "You're kidding, right?"

"No, of course I'm not," I said. "I said that I could tell you anything. Well, that's the biggest anything I know. You aren't shocked or horrified, I hope." I said *that* part lightly, kiddingly.

"No," she said. "I guess I'm really flattered. And I like *you* a whole lot, too. Can I tell you . . . well, just about *my* biggest anything?"

"Naturally," I said. "We're intimate. I want you to."

"Well," she said, "at first I thought you were a dweeb. Cute-looking, but a dweeb. I *always* thought you were real cute."

"I know the rest," I said. "You wanted me to help you with your Spanish. You were going to use me. And, at the same time, show your mother you had friends who were . . . respectable."

"Yeah!" she said. "How did *you* know? And then you treated me so nice and all, it got so I was liking you. I saw how much I owed you, too."

"You don't owe me anything," I said.

"No?" she said. "It seemed to me I did."

"Uh-uh," I said. "That isn't how it works. Not when two people love each other, when they're meant to be together, like we are."

"*Meant* to?" Mary said. "How d'you mean?"

That was the time for me to tell her—*a* time, anyway. Tell her I'd been told to help her out, to save her life. Explain to her how we'd been thrown together by a friendly force we couldn't understand—call it fate, or God, good luck, whatever. I'm not sure exactly why I didn't. Maybe I decided it was more than she could handle—too metaphysical or something, for the freshman mind. Or possibly I thought she'd find it *un*romantic, and think I didn't love her for herself, that I was only following orders in all this.

"Oh, I don't know," I said. "It's just this real good feeling that I have. That everything's so perfect. That loving one another's so completely natural. *You* know what I mean."

We pulled up outside her house just as I was finished saying that. I undid my seat belt. Mary was looking straight ahead.

"You *do* know, right?" I said to her.

She turned toward me. "Golly, *I* don't know," she said. "I haven't had, like, the *experience* you've had. You're a senior. Next year, you'll be in *college*. I'm still . . . meeting people, having fun. I guess I'd *like* to be like you. Be totally responsible and everything. Know all about what's in the *news* and stuff. But now . . ." She shook her head, looked down between the bucket seats.

"It doesn't matter," I said hastily. "We love each other; that's what counts. These other things *evolve*." She couldn't tell *me* that she didn't love me. She'd *shown* me that she did, enthusiastically and artlessly; no words could say it better. "Look, we'll take it slow. I know you have this other . . . well, commitment that may take a while before it gets *unraveled*. In the meantime, we can see each other here a little bit—and maybe up at my place." I'd fix my parents somehow. "Right?"

"Oh, *yeah*," she said. Her eyes came up to mine, and I filled up with love and tenderness. She looked near tears, I thought.

"Thanks for a *really* lovely time," she said. "I liked your place a lot." Then she leaned forward, pecked me quickly on the lips, and bolted out the door, her bookpack in her hand.

I took a moment to—as the saying goes—collect myself. It seemed as if a lot of stuff was loose inside my head, and flying here and there. Good stuff, not-so-good-or-unresolved stuff, stuff I didn't fully understand, stuff I had to work on, voices, *ecstasy*. It felt more complicated, being me, than ever in my life before.

14

IT WAS sheer luck my mother didn't see me coming in the house that late, late afternoon. I had forgotten to put *packages* inside the car, ahead of time. If she had got me in her sights, she surely would have asked me how the shopping went. With nothing in my hands, I would have had to say it hadn't gone at all, or pretended that I'd gotten only diamond studs and Chapsticks, little things that I had hidden in my pockets.

I went straight upstairs to my room, undressed, and took a shower. While I was doing that, I thought of Mary for a little while, and then of Tara. These different thoughts had very opposite effects on me. I decided that, at some point later on that night, I'd call up Tara. I didn't want to face her on the bus, cold turkey, knowing who was penciled in to play the turkey.

Trying to think what I would say to her was bad enough, but I had other stressful items on my mind as well. Our family has just one number and three telephones. These are in my parents' bedroom, and the kitchen, and the barn. I also have two parents, one of whom, my mother, goes in and out of the kitchen forty-seven times a night. She also stays up late, much later than my dad, because she doesn't have a part to play in morning milking nowadays. I didn't want to use the *barn* extension to call Tara; that would be too weird and, if discovered, lead to many comments and/or questions, maybe Pentothal injections, up the line.

It occurred to me that being my age was unbearable. If you don't have relationships, you're bummed; you know your parents wonder why. But if you do, you're almost double-bummed. Your parents want to stick their noses into them. And, unlike your parents' marriage, *your* relationships are *complicated*, full of ups and downs, confusions and uncertainties. Relationships, the ones you don't have *or* the ones you're having, are about the *last* thing that a guy my age would choose to dwell on with his parents. At that point in time, I simply *hated* being seventeen, in love with fourteen, loathed (I'd bet a dollar) by another seventeen. I was furious I didn't have a phone up in my room; that seemed *outrageous* and *unfair*. I'd forgotten that I'd never needed one before.

Mom asked about my Christmas shopping at the dinner table. I wiggled out of answering by telling her I'd gotten lumps of coal and switches all around, which was what *her* mom had said that Santa would bring *me*, when I was small and bugging her about my presents. I was back up in my room, as usual, shortly after we had finished eating.

I didn't start my homework right away, however. Instead, I lay down on my bed and thought about that afternoon, and Mary. It had been unreal. As a marker on the road to adult life, the happenings that day would have to rank with learning how to drive a tractor, anyway. New horizons now had opened up before me. Possi-*proba*-bilities. No rush to get there, either. Love can take its own, sweet time. I'd had some feedback on my body, on my . . . sexuality, I guess. And it was—it had been—*good!*

I got up off my bed and went over to the bookcase where

my tape deck was. There, I played the relevant section of the "Steam It Open" tape a bunch of times, at real low volume, kneeling on the floor and punching "play" and "rewind," and then "play" again. "Save her life," the voice demanded. I thought it held an urgency I hadn't heard before.

"Yes," I started answering. "I damn well *will*."

"I promise you," I said as I rewound.

"Oh, Mary, yes, of course I will," I answered.

It didn't sound like Mary on the tape. I just liked to say her name a lot.

When I finally turned the tape deck off, it hit me it was *Thursday* night, and that both my parents were upstairs, already in their bedroom. Their Thursday-night routine was different—yes, unique. Mom and Dad were both big fans of *Cheers*, the TV show, and my dad was willing to give up a half an hour's sleep to watch it—but in bed. Sometimes I'd go in and watch it with them. In any case, they'd turn the light out after. It was the one night of the week that both of them were out of circulation by nine-thirty.

That was excellent. I gave them twenty minutes more to fall asleep, and then, on little cat feet, made my way downstairs, and to the kitchen. My palm was slick with sweat, as I picked up the telephone.

Tara answered. "Hi," I said. "It's Shep."

"Oh, hi," she said. Just that.

I did a little unplanned nervous laughing.

"I guess you were surprised to see me in the car with Mary there, this afternoon," I said.

"Sort of," she said, sort of coolly. "There aren't all that many freshman dentists, I don't think."

I used another hee-haw.

"Obviously, I didn't go to the dentist," I said. I was speaking fast, and softly, and (I hoped) sincerely. "When I told you I was going, I was lying. And I lied to you before. When I told you there was nothing going on—with Mary and myself, *between* us? Well, there was and is." I paused to take a breath. "Something. Going on."

"I see," said Tara. "I more or less *assumed* that was the case. But I guess I don't see why you didn't tell me when I asked you. That really kind of bugs me. Isn't that what having friends is all about? *Sharing* things with one another? Especially . . . well, *heartfelt* things?"

I groaned inside.

"Yes, of course. I *know* it is," I said. "I don't know *why* I didn't tell you." Except, of course, I did. Why couldn't I admit it? Why did I have to tell *another* lie? How high would they build up? "I'm just a liar and a jerk, I guess."

"But—that's exactly what you're *not*," said Tara. "I've known you all my life. You never have been either of those things."

" 'Something is as Something does,' " I said, quoting confusedly from the-truth-according-to-my-mother.

"Uh-uh," said Tara. "You *could* lie. And I guess you did. But Shepherd Catlett ain't no liar."

She was being so damn nice, I almost couldn't stand it. What I wanted—needed and deserved—was coals of fire.

"I didn't used to be," I said. "But lately . . . *I* don't know. I *am, have been*. I wouldn't blame you if you didn't want to have a thing to do with me."

"Piffle," Tara said. Where she gets her words sometimes I do not know. "You don't get rid of me that easily." (Was *that* what I'd been trying to do? I asked myself. *Oh, no*. Or I don't *think* so, anyway.) "This is something major in your life, and so I care about it. In fact, what I just thought was, if *you* like

Mary Sutherland so much, she must be really special. So, if you don't mind, I'd like to get to know her—and to like her—too."

That threw me for a loop.

"She thinks you're really pretty," popped into my mind, and so I said it. Out of desperation? Maybe.

Tara laughed. "Well, there's a good place to begin," she said. "I'll take her to an oculist."

"Hey, cut it out," I said. I'd suddenly relaxed a little. "Don't start up again with that. I *told* you you were gorgeous. That's what *everybody* thinks. You just don't like to hear me say it."

"Don't I?" Tara said. "Maybe I ..." But then she said, "Forget it. But—hey, wait ... before you go, hang up I mean, I've got something to tell *you*."

I don't know why, but when she said that, I took one quick breath and held it. I had no idea what she was going to say, but somehow—for some reason—I was terrified.

"My mother's had a major change of schedule at work," she said. Mrs. Garza was the bookkeeper at that immense new Grand Union supermarket. "They're putting some new system in—some new computer deal or something, I don't know. And lots of things are getting switched around. So, anyway, they want her there at eight now, and I told her I'd ride in with her. She seemed to want the company. I *know* she will, as soon as it gets snowy. So, anyway, starting with tomorrow, I won't be on the bus, not going, anyway." There was a pause. "I didn't want you worrying, or anything."

"Well, thanks for telling me," I said. My mind was whirling, trying to sort that out.

"I didn't think you'd want to go with us," she added. "If *I* were you, I wouldn't."

"Well," I said again, "let's see." I thought I saw, already. "No. You'd have to start out going in the wrong direction. I wouldn't want you doing that. And anyway, that'd be too early, seeing I do morning milking. As it is, I just have time. You know—to eat and all."

"Mmm," said Tara. "And as far as coming back, I'm not sure *what* I'll do. I think I may come back with Mom at first. Just to show an interest in her life. That'll give her one less thing to bitch about. Or it'll let her do her bitching early and avoid the rush."

When I didn't comment right away, she added, "But I'll be seeing you in school."

"Oh, sure," I said. "I understand." We hung up shortly afterward. I don't know; I *might* have understood—or not. I wasn't all that confident. I went upstairs to try to do some homework.

But when I got upstairs, I lay down on my bed again, and thought some more. Tara'd sounded super-nice—and reasonable—but maybe she was lots more steamed at me than she was letting on. Maybe her idea was to get to know Mary so's to tell her what a *re*tard jerk I'd always been, and what a liar I was now. Maybe *she* had talked her mother into heading down to Burnside early, just so that she wouldn't have to deal with me that much.

One thing seemed pretty sure: That plan of mine to go to Dustin with her and do early Christmas shopping was *kaput*. I wouldn't have the nerve to ask her to do that for me. Which meant the lie I'd told my mother would remain in place, full-sized and undiminished. Life, my life, had sure been *tarnished* lately.

I did a pretty half-assed job on that damn homework, too.

15

I FELT STRANGE next morning, on the bus. It slowed, approaching Tara's house, but never stopped; the seat beside me stayed unoccupied. I got the feeling fellow riders noticed that, and took to whispering among themselves, asking one another what I'd done to Tara.

Neither of the Delberts was on board, but everyone was used to that. They hadn't made the bus since Melchiorre beat up Dwayne. I wondered if they ever would come back to school; both of them were old enough so that they didn't have to. I thought that maybe I would write a terse description of the attack and send it to either Mr. Reese or the school paper, if nothing seemed to be happening by the end of the week. It was too bad Tara wasn't there, I thought; we could have talked that idea over. Lots had been accomplished on our bus rides, through the years. Many of my thoughts, ideas, opinions, attitudes, had first emerged aboard the big banana. Some of them, I'd borrowed from my seatmate, too. I guess I felt a little . . . *jilted*. "Something old, something new, some things borrowed, someone blue," I thought. The mild originality of that—I am not a terribly creative person—made me feel a little better.

School that day was nowhere near the same as usual. For one thing, I was close to being unprepared, by my standards. So, deprived of my accustomed security blanket, I behaved ... oh, *furtively,* I guess—not looking at the teacher much, bringing one hand up to do a lot of brief massages on my forehead and my eyebrows.

Spanish, though, was different; I didn't have to sweat the Spanish. Also, Spanish class had Mary in it. Looking at her during class, I remembered a line from a romance novel that my mother read out loud one time, to Dad and me: "His eyes devoured her." I'd laughed that day, along with my progenitors, but there in Spanish class I didn't laugh at all. Instead— don't *you* laugh, now—I felt my mouth begin to water. I *wanted* to "devour" Mary, absolutely, any parts or all of her. After class, the two of us exchanged the briefest "Hi's," but looking in her eyes became the high point of my day.

Later, on my way to Modern European History, I saw her once again, walking up the hall—with Tara! Even though I'd been forewarned, that jolted me. They looked so ... natural together. And, later still, from out of the bus window ... there they were again, coming down the front steps of the school, chatting up a storm! The only thing they had in common—so it seemed to me—was *me*. Were they telling each other "everything" already—the way that girls are said to do? Or was this Queen Tara's show? If so, then Mary *could* be hearing juicy bits of Shepherd's history. Perhaps including what a lying little *shit* the guy was turning out to be.

That night, after supper, I snuck into my parents' room and called up Mary. Although it was a Friday, I hadn't given half a minute's thought, all day, to trying to get a date that night. In my mind, there was a linkage now, between myself and Mary. Although I *could* go out with other girls, it seemed ridiculous and meaningless to do so.

Mary's mother answered: "Yes?"

"Oh, Mrs. Sutherland, hello," I said, relaxed and confident. "It's Shepherd Catlett."

"Who?" she said. I heard a man's voice in the background, or TV.

"Shepherd *Catlett*," I repeated. "Mary's friend. I came for dinner last week?" Pause. "On Tuesday?" Pause. "We had the chicken?"

"Oh, *Shep!*" she said. "Hello! I swear, this telephone's been acting funny for a week. I think it must be wearing out, Mary uses it so much." I remembered that there wasn't any TV in the living room.

"Gee, I've never heard of that," I said. "Of course, I guess it's possible."

"I think I mentioned it to Mary," said her mother. "It seemed to me she would have noticed the same thing. But, as I recall, she hadn't."

"Well," I said, "that's interesting." Liar. "Actually, I was hoping I could have a word with her. With Mary? Is she home?"

"Mary?" said her mother. "No. No, no she isn't. Now, let's see. Tonight she's baby-sitting for some people named Vermillion—isn't that a funny name?—over on the other side of town. I'd say that you could call her over there, except they haven't got a telephone. Peculiar, in this day and age, but there you are. I've heard some people think it gives off harmful rays, the telephone. And when you come to think about it, well, why shouldn't that be true?" I heard the background voice again.

"I suppose . . ." I said, not knowing what to say.

"So, is there any message, Shep?" she asked.

"No," I said. "Except . . . if you'd just tell her that I called?

I'll try her in the morning, if you think that that'd be all right."

"Oh, absolutely," she replied. "Just not too early, though. We like to get our beauty sleeps, on Saturdays and Sundays." And she laughed.

"Sure," I said. I wanted to get off the phone. "I understand. Well, thanks a lot, then, Mrs. Sutherland. Good-bye."

"Bye-bye, Shep, dear," she said. "Sleep tight." And both of us hung up.

Next morning, I helped out my dad, first in the barn, then outside, spreading some manure. After that I volunteered to prune the apple trees, a job I didn't like that much, but which would put me near the house, so's I could use the phone.

I waited till eleven-thirty. Phooey. Mrs. Sutherland again.

"Oh, *Shep!* Good *morning*, dear," she said. "Isn't it a *lovely* day outside?"

I said it was. I was going to make the best of it, of everything. "And it sounds as if I didn't wake you." I laughed at the absurdity of that. It was almost lunchtime, after all.

"No, you didn't," she agreed. "But that's just me. Mary, *she's* our little sleepyhead. I've known *her* to stay tucked in till one or two P.M. on weekends, if you can believe it."

"You mean she's still asleep?" I said. Of course, it's true: Different people need varying amounts of sleep. Thomas Edison, supposedly, hardly slept at all.

"Well, I think I heard her stirring, just a little bit ago," her mother said. "Let me find out. I know she'd want to speak to *you*. Hold on a second, Shep, while I run up and see what's going on."

I could have run up Coffin's Hill and partway down again while I was waiting, with the phone pressed hard against my ear. At one point, I came close to hanging up, thinking Mary's batty mother had forgotten me.

Then, suddenly, "H'lo? Hi, Sh'p." It almost certainly was Mary, sounding pretty much as if the novocaine had not worn off.

"Hey, hi," I said, a little loud and probably a lot too cheerful. "How you doing? Hope your mother didn't wake you up." Silence, so I added, "It's eleven forty-*five,* y'know."

"Mmmph," she said. "I know. She *said.* It's just . . . let's see. I got home really late. The people I was sitting for . . . *you* know. They didn't, like, come home till . . . really, really late." I heard her yawn.

"Yeah, sure," I said. "I'm sorry. Go on back to bed. But, first"—I started talking fast, and much, much softer—"I was wondering if, possibly this afternoon—much later on, I mean—if I was in the neighborhood, could I, well, possibly stop by, for just a little while? And say hello, and maybe"— nervous laugh—"we could listen to some music, or whatever." I laughed again, but this one had a tinge of . . . naughtiness in it.

I'm sure I wasn't kidding either one of us. What I wanted was "whatever," and I believe that she did, too—whatever that turned out to be. I could imagine—even *visualize*— some possibilities.

"Mmm. Well, see, the thing is, yeah, I'd really like that, Shep, except I *can't,*" she finally said, still sounding kind of fuzzy. "I'm meeting . . . well, my *girlfriend*—you remember that I told you, she's the one I went down to the clinic with? And, well, we've gotta do some stuff—or *she* does, really— an' you see, I promised her I'd *stay* with her and then, like, after, *you* know, *be* with her—sleep over at her house an' all—in case she needed me, or anything."

"Oh," I said. Heavy disappointment hit me in the gut. The excitement I'd been feeling limped away. "Well, that's too bad. . . . I was kind of hoping that, *you* know, we'd have a chance . . . It's just I'm missing you already, loving you so much, and all. I don't suppose that *Sunday*—"

She didn't let me finish. But now she sounded much more like my girl, more wide awake.

"Oh, Shep, honey, *no*. I can't plan *anything* this weekend, really—'cept for her," she said. "I *really* want to see you, too. Just talking on the phone with you's enough to make me . . . *you* know." And she chuckled. "But I *promised* Beth, I really did." She paused. "But how about . . . now let me think a second. How about . . . next Thursday or Friday *afternoon,* either one of those? Friday might be better, actually. I *think* we'd have the house all to ourselves on Friday after school— that might be fun. It seems to me my mom is . . . How about we say right now? Friday, after school?"

"Great," I said. Excitement ran back in and jumped up on my lap. The house all to *ourselves*? "That sounds superb." No longer did I even think about a car, the chores, my parents' attitudes; I was simply *going* for it, *doing* it. "I'll see you Friday, then. As well as in ol' *Español.*" I suddenly remembered something else. "And by the way, I saw you with my neighbor, Tara—Tara Garza?—yesterday. The girl that waved when we were driving out to my place?"

"Tara, yeah," said Mary. "What about her?"

"Nothing—just that I kept *seeing* you with her," I said. "I thought you didn't know her."

"Well, I didn't," Mary said. "But now I do. She actually came up to me and introduced herself." By now she sounded totally awake. "She's really nice. She said she's known you all her life. Like, ever since the two of you were *babies*!"

"That's true," I said. "She's always been just like a sister to me."

"I know. You would have been embarrassed if you'd heard what-all she said about you," Mary said. "It was really cute. You would have turned beet red."

I decided to assume the best. "We've always been real pals," I said. "Tara's solid as a rock—and smart." I'd made her sound as if she were a St. Bernard, or possibly an elephant.

"*I* thought so," Mary said. "Sometimes I think I'd like to have an older sister. Someone pretty much like her. But then I think 'Forget it.' Mom is bad enough, the way she tries to stick her nose in all my business."

"Tell me about it," I said carelessly. "Parents can't leave well enough alone."

"Whatever that means," Mary said, and laughed. "So, anyway. I gotta go and take my shower now. I guess I'm up, no getting out of it. Thanks for calling, Shep. And, mmm— I'm looking forward now, to Friday."

"Great," I said again. "I love you, Mare." I hung up with a flourish.

So, Saturday passed pleasantly enough. I started working on a paper that'd be due in my English class before the Christmas holiday. I'd decided on my topic: "Shakespeare: Feminist or MCP?" I was going to base it on the plays we'd studied in my English classes, starting in ninth grade: *The Merchant of Venice, Macbeth, Hamlet,* and *King Lear.* Starting out, I was leaning toward "feminist," based on all the potent women in those plays, but knowing me, I also figured that I'd end up in the safety zone of middle ground. I tend to do that, not go out on limbs. Repeating: I am not a troublemaker.

Sunday also was okay. I surprised my mom by saying that I'd like to go to church with her, if she was going. The thing was, I'd decided loving Mary wasn't just a physical phenomenon. Love, my love for her, had other ... aspects. I felt protective of her, thankful *for* her; I felt a bit transformed myself—if you can follow that. God, I thought, might be a part of all those feelings; they transcended ordinary (music-loving, *Time*-subscribing) Shepherd Catlett. I thought it wouldn't hurt if I sat down with God and acted friendly for a while. I figured that God *knew* I'd never ruled God out—even when I wasn't hanging out with him-or-her.

And so I went, and it was nice. I expressed a lot of heartfelt gratitude and asked for any further help that I might qualify for. I said I'd surely "save her life" if called upon to do so—or at least I'd *try*.

I didn't hear an *answer*, there at church, but at lunchtime there were questions—from a (surely) lesser being.

"So, how come you went to church?" my other father asked, while carving Sunday chicken. He often doesn't go himself, that day for instance.

"I had my reasons," I said cagily. "But, at this time, I'd like to plead the Fifth."

"Oh, you lawyers—" he began.

"The Fifth *Commandment*," I broke in to say.

He furrowed up his brow. "Let's see," he said. "That implies you've started going out with *married* women, right?"

"*Please*," I said. "You're thinking of the Seventh, Dad. The Fifth"—I dropped my eyes—"is 'Honor thy father and thy mother.' "

That earned me grudging admiration. "Oh," he said. "Hee. Haw."

I smiled the victor's modest smile and asked for the potatoes.

Monday, nothing happened in particular. Tuesday, Tara dropped the bomb, a Big Boy.

We had met for lunch, as usual. She led me to the far end of an empty table, where she sat down hard and stared at me.

"Mary's heading for big trouble, Shep," was how it started.

"Mary?" I said stupidly. Suddenly, the thermal top that I was wearing felt real tight.

"Yes, Mary. Mary *Sutherland*," she said. She sounded angry. "Those stories I was telling you before? They're true. She's hanging out with sewer rats and rattesses. And *they* are—what's the quaint old phrase?—they're *using* her. She's drinking much too much and getting treated like . . . oh, I don't know. Let's say some kind of *toy*."

"No," I said. I put the sandwich I'd begun unwrapping back down on the table. Then I put it back inside the paper bag. I didn't have an appetite. I had the opposite of appetite. "I don't believe it. Even if that *was* true once, it isn't anymore."

"Wrong," said Tara. "I know it's true because she told me. Some of it last week, and more today. *She* thinks she's having fun, walking on the wild side, living on the edge. That kind of crap."

"A lot of kids do alcohol," I said. "It's sort of like a *whadyacallit*—rite of passage." That's what *Time* had said.

Tara shook her head. "Not the way she's doing it," she said. "She's getting bombed three nights a week—Wednesdays, Fridays, and Saturdays. With Gerry and the boys, and some carefully selected females. A lot of them are cheerleaders."

Of course, I thought about how Mary'd sounded at eleven forty-five on Saturday.

"They drink and . . . party," Tara said. "Every party has a theme. Mary said the next one's going to be a Roman orgy. Wine from wicker bottles. Everybody's got to put a toga on."

I made a face. "I can't believe this," I kept saying. "Mary's still fourteen. . . ."

"She says the drinking's in her genes," said Tara. "And she thinks most girls would kill to be in her shoes, hanging out with seniors, having fun with just about the coolest guys in school." Tara hadn't touched her sandwich, either.

"So, how did you respond to all of this?" I asked. "To all these *revelations*." It wasn't fair, but I was sounding mad—at Tara, for giving me this news. And for not, well, *fixing* everything. She surely knew how totally beyond me all this was.

Instead of looking sympathetic, she appeared disgusted. "Just the way you'd think," she said. "I told her she was playing dangerous games. That, frankly, it upset me. That she made me think a lot of *me*, a side of me I wasn't all that crazy about. But I also told her that I couldn't run her life for her. At the end, she said, 'Just don't tell Shep, all right?' but I told her that I couldn't promise that."

I nodded. I was feeling totally messed up, furious at Gerry and that bunch, and at Mary. And in a funny way, myself. But I also loved her, Mary, more than ever, feeling her . . . *endangered*, as I did.

"Well, I'm going to talk to her," I said. "I won't let her go to any 'Roman orgy' party." How could Gerry Mays know anything about a Roman orgy, anyway, that *moron*.

Tara said, "The dumbest thing that you could do is start to give her orders. Push her, and she'll dig her heels in, just the same as I would."

The trouble with a lot of good advice is that it's what you know already, put in words. Which means you can't stand hearing it.

"Well, tough," I said. I didn't look her in the eye. "So where's the party going to be?"

"I don't know," said Tara, and now she sounded pretty well fed up. "And if I did, I wouldn't tell you, Shep. You've got a chance to really help this girl—she *likes* you. The fact that she's so young is good; that means she . . ."

But I was on my feet and, out of habit, picking up the paper bag that had my untouched lunch inside it.

"I can't sit here and not do *something*," I informed her icily. "I appreciate your telling me, and your advice, but clearly you don't see . . ."

Even as I spoke those words, I knew she did—and all too well. I suppose the trouble was that I was too confounded, too confused, for words—for *any* words, whether they were hers or mine. I had no plan or course of action in my mind, except to move, get out of there, find Mary, scream, or kill someone—or *something*, as I said.

Turning from the table, I heard Tara's angry voice behind me. "So, go ahead," she said. "Go prove you really *are* a jerk. . . ."

16

OF COURSE I went and looked for her. If I'd found her, God knows what I would have said or done.

But that's another story. Or, to be more blunt, another lie.

Under the spell of Tara's and my own advice, I doubtless would have pleaded with her. I would have lain down in her path, the way a lot of self-styled saviors of other sorts have lain down in the paths of bulldozers and trucks and trains. And probably, like some of them, I would have been run over.

Or maybe she would have stopped for me, or turned off in some other, sensible direction.

Who *was* I trying to kid? Why, me, of course, who else? Just me.

You probably have guessed I didn't find her. I really didn't know her schedule, for one thing. I did do something pretty shrewd, however. I found out where the Roman orgy would be happening, on Wednesday night.

Here's Shepherd being slick as glass:

"Hey—lookin' forward to the Roman thing tomorrow night," I said to Amy Golden, the Laura Dern–like cheerleader, who actually was in my English class.

"*You're* going?" she inquired. Her expression fought and lost a battle with I-can't-believe-it.

"Sure," I said. "I thought I might slide by. Gerry said his mother's place. That'd be the house on Cedar, right?"

"Uh-uh," she said, and laughed. "That's Gerry's *dad's*. You wouldn't want to show up there—not looking like old Nero and the boys. His mom's is over on South Prospect. Number ninety-two, I think it is—back off the road."

"Oh, yeah, of course," I said. "See you there, then, Amy. 'Weenie, weedie, weekie,' right?" I did my best to leer.

And, you know, I think I might have, too. Skepticism and amazement, both, left Amy's face, to be replaced (I thought) by a kind of a coquettish grin.

"Maybe we'll find out. I'll see ya, Shep," she said.

After school, I walked to Mary's house.

There I rang the doorbell; nothing happened, so I pounded on the door.

Then I turned away, and hitchhiked home.

Wednesday, I bolted out of History right at the bell and quick-stepped through the halls to Spanish. The conversation that I'd had with Tara had worn off. I was mad that Mary hadn't been at home the day before. My mood was presidential; I was ready to kick A.

I checked inside the room. She wasn't there, so I took up my post right by the door. The trouble was, she seldom got there until right before the bell—and of course that day was no exception.

I spotted her approaching. She saw me and slowed. I moved in her direction.

"Hi," I said. "We've got to talk." Original.

She smiled, but not convincingly. "So, talk," she said.

I said, "I heard about the party. The Roman orgy one. At Gerry's."

124

She gave a little shrug and stuck with "So?"

"You going to it?" I demanded to know. I'm afraid "demanded" *is* the word for what I did.

"I don't know. I thought I might," she said.

I stepped up closer to her and lowered my voice. Only later did I realize I sounded like my mother sounded—*used to* sound, *did* sound a time or two—when she was molding me (my character, I guess) some years ago.

"It doesn't sound like such a hot idea to *me*," I hissed. "Getting into all that drinking, with that bunch of *jerks*. . . ."

"They're friends of mine," she said. "I have a lot of different friends. You're not the only person that I know, you know."

I recognized her tone of voice. It was defensive, heading into hostile. I was hearing someone digging in her heels.

"I absolutely *know* that," I insisted, trying (almost surely much too late) to switch from hot to cool. "But because I *am* a friend of yours, a friend"—I whisper-muttered this—"who *loves* you, Mary, I don't want to see you—"

"Oh, come off it, Shep," she said. "You're trying to tell me what to do. That's bullsh—"

"Señorita y señor!" Señora Markham had come up behind us. *"Entres, por favor!"* She held the classroom door for us.

Of course I marched right in. It was only when I'd gotten to my seat I saw that Mary hadn't followed.

Her doing that—or, actually, *not* doing that—plain ticked me off. I decided if she didn't want to deal with me, I didn't want to deal with her. To hell with her. Who did she think she was, the little snot?

From the end of Spanish class until I got on the bus, I didn't say a word to anyone. I ate my lunch outside alone, and when I walked the halls from one class to the next, I kept my eyes down, seeing nothing but the floor in front of me, and legs below the knee. If anybody—people—wanted to accost me, they were welcome to, but I wasn't initiating anything. Nor did I want to see who went from here to there with whom, or what relationships . . . were forming.

When I got on the bus, Mrs. Bates seemed glad enough to see me, even pleased to drive me home.

That didn't change my message, my reaction, to the day: "Frankly, everyone at Burnside High, Shepherd doesn't give a damn."

Arriving home, I had to suck it up and try to act in ways that both my parents would perceive as "normal." Turned out it wasn't all that hard, because the first thing that I did when I got back was change my clothes and head out to the barn. And there, the animals . . . well, *mellowed* me. As usual.

I wouldn't try to kid you. Sure, a cow—or cows—will get me mad sometimes. In general, they aren't any smarter than, say, Mr. Melchiorre, which means that some of them do dumb, annoying things occasionally—involving, as a rule, body wastes, or feet, or tails. But they also can be awfully sweet and gentle and accommodating. And because, unlike some other farmers, we give names to all our cows, each member of the herd is almost like a pet, a member of the family.

Beside the cows, we have three cats that hang around the barn, and Ace, our semi–Border collie, is on duty there at every milking, ready with a smile for me and waiting (with unbated breath) for the next fantastic, ego-building, smoothly executed cattle drive.

So, within an hour of my getting home, I was feeling much, much better, and I hardly had to "act" at all, in order to appear myself. It was only when I let my thoughts veer back to school, and Mary, that I'd feel an awful, sinking feeling—where my stomach met my heart, I guess.

After supper, when I went upstairs and started doing homework, it got harder *not* to think about the feelings that I'd had—*still* had—for Mary. I couldn't just stop loving her; I didn't even *want* to. I thought of how she'd looked and acted in the backseat of my mother's car; I remembered how she'd said that she was looking forward to our date on Friday afternoon, and how we'd have that nice brick house "all to ourselves."

Shortly after I began to study Physics—there was going to be a unit test the next day—my eyes fell on the tape deck near my desk. *Thud*—the sinking feeling hit me hard again. *If* my function (purpose/duty) was to "save her life," I wasn't doing much of a job of it (at this point in time). How could I just sit there, making sure I got another 90 on another stupid test, while the life in question was, if not in jeopardy, at least not being valued and respected?

Answer: Obviously, I couldn't. Not if I was going to be a . . . well, "good" Shepherd.

I got up and went downstairs. With utter casualness, I told my parents that I'd promised Tara to come over to her house and study Physics with her, for the test. "Okay to take the Buick?" I asked Mom.

She nodded affably, of course. Extra study, with a neighbor (and a good one), was a yes-yes.

"Don't wait up," I said to her. "I may be pretty late."

"That's fine. Don't worry, dear," she said.

I waved my Physics book at them and headed for the door, picking up her keys in the front hall, along the way.

17

I DIDN'T have much trouble finding Gerry's mother's house. Although you couldn't see its number, 92, from Prospect Street, you *could* see number 86 before you got to it, and then a house set off the road, with three cars in the driveway, and another three in front of it. I parked across the street, with the Buick pointed in the opposite direction. Then, on foot, I double-checked the number on the house *beyond* the house set off the road and found that it was 98. That meant I *had* found Gerry's mother's place, all right. It was big, and sat there on what looked to be at least an acre lot.

So, now I had to *do* something. Driving down from Highridge Road, I'd tried to figure out the moves that I would make. Once I got beyond the total fantasies (in which, for instance, I just kicked the door down, ordered everyone to freeze, scooped Mary up with easy grace, and left a live grenade on the front porch as I departed), nothing really sprang to mind. The only constant while I thought about my doing anything was how my heart kept pounding, and my chest did not have room for any real deep breath. And how my hands kept slipping wetly on the steering wheel.

Arriving, I decided I would take a look around.

Bent over in a crouch, I started up the far side of the driveway, keeping cars between me and the house. There was music coming from inside, but at a level that would not offend the neighbors. It offended (but at the same time pleased) *me*, though. The album that was playing when I first arrived was one by Billy Joel. Authentic Roman orgy music, right?

My task as scout was complicated by the fact that I couldn't see inside. Drapes and curtains had been drawn across all the downstairs windows; on the second floor, the shades were pulled in every room, it seemed. Lights went on and off—and on and off again—in different upstairs rooms while I was watching.

I loitered in that driveway more than half an hour, a lot of time just resting on one knee and leaning up against a fender. I suppose that I was stalling. I preferred to think of it as waiting for a *happening*—something on the order of a burning bush, let's say—a *sign*. The landing of a UFO would certainly have been acceptable. Anything I could *react* to. I've mentioned my accepting nature, haven't I? Farmers are *muy* patient, too.

But no signs were forthcoming. I finally left the shelter of the first car in the line, ducked around a cedar hedge, and found myself behind the house. There, there were some flower beds, the usual back lawn, and a sizable brick outdoor fireplace that I could kneel in back of, if I wanted to. I did, although (again) I didn't think to pray. Now I was staring at a little open porch, connected to what surely was the back, or kitchen, door.

I supposed that that would be the door for me to use, if I went in. *When* I went in, that is.

But before I even started counting down to that event, it opened, with a creak, and out of the interior darkness came two people. Once on the porch, they perched there, on its railing. In the dimness of the starlight, I recognized them both: Max Edelman and Jenny Foss. They both had glasses in their hands and were dressed incongruously in outdoor boots and parkas over their pathetic pseudo-togas. Jenny's was at least a solid color, maybe peach, but the sheets in Max's house, apparently, all came in boldly colored geometric patterns.

While I looked on, Max fished out cigarettes and held a match for both of them. (Well, I thought, at least there's *one* thing Gerry's mother won't permit inside her house.) They smoked and drank and said a few things that I couldn't hear. Eventually, they flicked their butts away and clomped back in. Jenny stumbled as she crossed the threshold, bouncing off the doorframe into Max. I heard the sound of something splashing on the floor, and both of them began to giggle.

Another set of minutes passed. I was beginning to relax. That was partly due to seeing Max and Jenny in the stupid flesh, I thought; "familiarity breeds contempt," I thought. Before I thought again, I rose up to my feet, made my way across the lawn, mounted the porch steps, and tried the door. It creaked again, but opened easily.

I stepped inside; I was in a little mudroom, with some boots and coats and skis.

The room beyond it was the kitchen, with only one small light on, right above the stove. I entered it.

It was an ordinary, good-sized kitchen: stove, a big refrigerator, a double sink, a lot of white steel cabinets, narrow back stairs going up, and two closed doors that could have led to closets or the basement. I tried them both, and it was one of each.

Through another open door, I could see a dining room. No lights were on in it, but a dim glow came from just beyond it, where the music and the party were. The living room, presumably. I crawled into the shadow underneath the sideboard and peered into the space beyond.

It was a party scene that I was looking at, all right, although the parties that I'd been to never had *evolved* as far as this one had. The ones I'd known were *kickball,* as compared to this, the major leagues.

Gerry's mother's living room was very big, with two fat couches in it, and I think another four large, cushioned, easy chairs—as well as tables, unlit standing lamps, and lots of floor space. Only one small table lamp was on, way over in one corner of the room.

As far as I could tell (looking slightly *up,* as I was doing), every couch and chair had, at the least, two bodies on it—although the only way I knew that they were living bodies (not just piles of body parts or bags of laundry) was that, from time to time, I saw them move. There was no way I could tell where Mary was.

She wasn't either of the people dancing—*sort* of dancing—anyway. Those were Max and Jenny, booted still, but parka-free, down to their designer togas. Both of those had managed to become undraped, however, and so had fallen off their upper bodies. Only the belts or sashes that they must have had around their waists had kept the things from falling to the floor. Although, in Jenny's case, hers couldn't have, regardless. Good ol' Max had pulled it up, in back, so he could hold her butt while they were dancing. In the dimness I could tell, if not as well as Max, that Jenny wasn't wearing any underwear.

I hate to admit it, but of course I gawked and gaped. Shamefully, my heart beat faster. Way beyond my depth? You bet I was—without a safety line, for sure.

"*Gaaah!* I swear, I drink another glass of this damn guinea red, I'm gonna puke!" It was a slurry voice from way across the darkness of the room, a guy. "Hey, Mary-sweets, you over near the door somewhere? How 'bout you get your buddy Tip a nice cold beer, a'right?"

No need to have a safety line to guide me. I crept back in the kitchen, fast, hopped inside the closet, and reclosed its door to just a crack.

I didn't hear her footsteps, coming in the room, but I did detect the sound of the refrigerator being opened. I pushed against the closet door and stepped into the room. Mary was bent over, peering in the fridge and reaching for a Molson's from the bottom shelf. She had on—I later noticed this— her seven finger rings, as usual. But nothing else, whatever.

"Christ," I said, involuntarily.

She turned around.

"Oh, *shit*," she said. I could tell that she was drunk. And then she started giggling. "You aren't dressed right . . . for the party, Shep."

At least I didn't say, "Like you are, I suppose." Instead, I took my jacket off and held it out to her.

"Put this on," I said.

She hesitated. Then she shrugged, put down the beer, and did as I had said. She even zipped the jacket up. It almost— barely—covered her; you know, the parts that should be covered, in the kitchen, ordinarily.

"You're coming home with me," I said, in a sort of a stage whisper. "You're getting out of here."

She seemed to think that over.

"I can't," she said. "My bag 'n stuff's upstairs. Besides, I'm havin' fun."

"You *think* you are," I said. "All you are's another little piece of ass to them." That last was so un-Shepherdish I barely could believe I'd said it.

"Bullshit," Mary said, and shook her head. "Gerry 'n Tipper love me jus's much as you do. Your trouble is, you wan' my boobs 'n stuff just for yourself, you . . . *hippa*crip. Don' tell *me* thatcha don'." She pulled the zipper of my jacket down again, to prove her point, I guess.

"That's not the point—" I started.

"Where the fuck's my beer?" said Tipper Doane, almost tripping on the sheet cinched 'round his waist, as he came in the kitchen.

"Hey, what's *Catlett* doin' here?" He said that louder—then got louder still. "Hey, Gerry! You ask Catlett to your party, man?"

What I suppose I should have done, right then, was grab ahold of Mary's arm and run like hell—drag her out the door and over to the Buick, shove her in and . . . drive three days to Reno and get married!

What I did instead was stand there looking (I imagine) like an indecisive dork, while most of the Roman orgy toga partiers came crowding in the kitchen to refresh their memories of what I looked like. It was certainly a sight we must have made: five bare-chested guys with different colored sheets (one floral-patterned) round their waists, four girls still busy wrapping other sheets across their chests and shoulders, Mary, naked, with my jacket gaping open still, and me, dressed like a farmer's son from up on Highridge Road.

"Just what the hell d'you think you're doing here?" asked Gerry Mays, on everyone's behalf.

"I'm taking Mary home," I told him.

"That's what you think, asshole," Gerry said. But then he smiled his famous scoring smile, and raised one hand, and

133

said, "But wait. Le's be completely fair." He turned and looked at Mary. "You want for asshole here to take you home?" He smiled. "Like that?"

Mary's eyes were glazed. She looked down at herself.

"Uh-uh," she said.

"Okay, then, give me asshole's jacket, an' then you and the other girls get back in the living room," said Gerry.

Mary took my jacket off and handed it to him. She didn't look at me. As she passed Gerry, following the other girls, he ran his hand right down her front—offhandedly, the way I'd pat a passing heifer.

"So, looks like you're the only one that's going," he then said to me. "Take your coat and get on outa here, you goddamn stumpjumper, before you get your ass kicked good." And with that he tossed my jacket at me.

I've said a bunch of times before that I am not a trouble-maker, and I'm not. I'm not a fighter, either. My parents brought me up nonviolently—that may be part of why I am the way I am, who knows? By now, I've intellectualized the issue. I've convinced myself that human beings, as a group, must see that fighting, as a way of settling disputes, is no longer . . . practical. Because we've come to be too good at killing one another, we are going to have to make all violence obsolete. I honestly believe that's going to happen, if there's going to be a not-too-distant future.

But at the moment I am speaking of, right now, that hasn't happened yet. I was not evolved enough. Gerry'd threatened me and called me names—a name—I very much despised. Also, I believed I had a cause—a love—I should defend, as (maybe) God had asked me to.

So what I did was growl, "Fuck you," and throw a leaping roundhouse right that landed high on Gerry Mays's left cheekbone.

What followed wasn't any sort of fight, measured against the ones you see in the movies, or on TV, where guys take turns knocking each other ass over teakettle, and throw people over their shoulders—and different ones go crashing into china cabinets, and sliding down the lengths of tables on their stomachs. I suppose this fight looked more like all the silly ones they have at baseball games, when all you see is a heap of squirming, flailing guys down on the ground.

My recollection of what happened isn't very good, but I believe the *second* punch I aimed at Gerry's head collided only with his shoulder, and that my momentum carried me right into him. And he, retreating, tripped, and I went down on top of him, while four more guys began to jump on, grab ahold of, punch, or kick me.

I think it was a struggle for a while. I had the motivation on them, and the conditioning, for sure—and I wasn't in the least impaired. Plus, I could try to kick or elbow, punch or knee, all parts of everyone I saw, and I had all the clothes on. But pretty soon they got some weight and grips on me, and I ran out of strength and energy, and started to absorb some really painful rockets, here and there. I remember trying to double up, protect my face and front (whatever looks et cetera I had), while somebody with boots just worked me over for a while. Then a great big flare exploded in my head and that was all I would remember.

(It all can sound so pat and easy when you write it down in words like that. In memory, it's very different, though. What passed in Gerry's mother's kitchen were, beyond a shadow of a doubt, the worst, most shameful, painful moments of my life.)

I came to lying in a field of scrubby second growth, not knowing where I was, or how I'd gotten there. I might have muttered "Mary" for some silly reason, but of course she wasn't there. Up on hands and knees, I looked around and saw that I was in an undeveloped lot, on Prospect Street, not all that far from Gerry's mother's house. When I made it to my feet, I took three steps toward number 92 and then fell down again, puking-sick and dizzy. I was finished as a savior—over, ended, beaten, done. Next time I struggled up, I headed for the Buick.

I was still God's chosen one to this extent, at least: I drove it safely home. My shock-resistant watch said twenty after one, when I arrived.

I opened the front door, and damned if my parents didn't come steaming out of the living room, both fully dressed.

"Good Lord," my mother said, and ran to me. "What's *happened* to you, Shep?" She started making standard mother-moves, I guess, reaching for my damaged face and head.

From behind her came my father's voice.

"Tara called a half an hour after you went out," he said. "She wanted you to come and study Physics. I took the truck and checked to see if you went off the road before you got to her place." It sounded like he almost wished he'd found me wrapped around a tree.

I wasn't feeling good at all, but I knew I could feel worse.

"I didn't go to Tara's and I got beat up," I said. "I don't want to talk about it. I just want to go to bed."

"But, Shep, your *face*," my mother said. "Don't be an idiot. Just let me—"

"Mother, *please*," I said. "Let me, for once . . . all right?"

I headed for the stairs. Out of the corner of one swollen eye, I'm pretty sure I saw my father put a hand out on my mother's shoulder. Thanks to the bannister, I made it to my room.

I went into the bathroom and cleaned up. My face looked worse than I'd expected—not badly cut, but swollen and abraded. I pressed an ice-cold washcloth up against it, here and there. My head ached something awful, but my pupils looked to be about the same as usual. I concluded that I didn't have a fractured skull and took some aspirin.

Before I got in bed, I found the "Steam It Open" tape and played it, right up past the place where I was told to "Save her life" again, as clear as ever.

I took the cassette out and laid it on my desk. Then I got a screwdriver and a hammer out of my little personal toolbox in the closet, and I opened up that cassette and pulled the tape out, off the reels.

I left it in a big brown jumble on the floor.

18

BREAKFAST WAS a bit of an ordeal. Before I came downstairs, I spent some fifteen minutes looking for the only pair of sunglasses I'd ever owned. When I put them on, they made the world seem even gloomier than I had known that it would be, the moment I woke up. My humiliated body ached all over, and I'd slept right through the morning milking.

So, Dad was in the barn still when I walked into the kitchen, looking like an ugly, ineffective, and untalented Tom Cruise.

"Morning, Mom," I said. I snagged a box of cold cereal and took it to my place.

"Good morning, dear," she said, but gravely. This made it clear to me we weren't going to have a normal morning.

I did the things that people do with cornflakes. The milk, seen through my shades, was gray.

"I'm not going to ask you anything about what happened," said my mom. "Or who else was involved. Or where you were. Or why you felt you had to lie to us."

She paused. I figured that those were, in fact, four questions, but I had no plans to answer them. I left them hanging in the empty, vaguely hostile air between us.

"But I really need to know—be sure—that you're all right," she said. "I take it that you plan to go to school?"

"That's right," I said, deciding as I said it.

"Well, I think you ought to go and let Dr. Peterkin—or whoever's on duty—take a look at you, as soon as you get into town," she said. "They open up at eight, you know."

"There's nothing wrong with me," I said, still looking at my cereal.

"I know, I know," she said. "But just to be completely on the safe side—"

"All right, I'll go," I said, to shut her up. I had no intention of so doing.

When my dad came in, he said, "Hey, look who's here—Mike Tyson," as if he'd spent time practicing the line.

I bared my teeth at him, knowing that he couldn't see my eyes.

"There's got to be a woman in the picture," he went on. "Like Mary Sutherland, for instance."

I shrugged my shoulders, one time, up and down.

"Although, to do all *that* much damage, she must have had a friend," he added with a chuckle.

I knew what he was doing, keeping it light so he wouldn't have to get into how angry he was at me for lying to them, which he didn't think I'd ever done before. Or not since I was grown up, anyway.

I stood up.

"I just can't talk about it right now," I said. "I'm sorry. Sorry that I can't, and sorry that I lied to you about where I was going. But"—I couldn't think of anything to say, for one long moment—"that's just the way it is," I finally finished.

I went upstairs and didn't come back down until my bus was almost due. When I stepped onto it, I said "Hello" to Mrs. Bates, but that was all I said to anyone, while on that trip to school.

Once there, I headed straight to English class, keeping my dark glasses on. Amy Golden came in after me. I didn't turn my head to look directly at her, but I still noticed she had changed (since leaving Gerry's mother's house) into a sweater, turtleneck, and jeans. I heard her whispering with someone, two rows back of me, getting out the word on how my face had been transformed, no doubt.

I took the Physics test. I knew a lot of what was on it, even though I hadn't really studied the material; I guessed at what I didn't know. It didn't matter what I got. I was ready when the bell rang. I handed in my paper and got out of there.

I heard Tara calling out my name. She was running down the hall after me, but I pretended that I didn't hear her, didn't know it. When she caught up and was walking along beside me, though, I turned to her before she had a chance to speak.

"I guess you want to gloat," I said. "You told me so. So, fine—you've done it. End of story. Good luck to both of you, you and your friend Mary. Oh, and thanks for tipping off my parents that I wasn't studying Physics, too."

All that came out dripping meanness, bile, hostility, you name it—all the stuff that slopped around my heart and mind. I knew I wasn't being fair, but right and not-right didn't matter in the least to me, not anymore.

Tara must have stopped and stood stock-still. Or something. In any case, she quickly wasn't there beside me anymore, and I was glad. I went and got my jacket from my locker, and then sat up in the stands outside and froze. I didn't read a book or anything.

Eventually, I went to Spanish class. Mary didn't try to talk to me, before or after, nor did she even turn her head toward me, as far as I could tell. She must have had a real bad hangover; she didn't look to be her stupid little carefree self.

As I got on the bus to head back home, I thought I saw her standing on the steps, again with Tara.

My mother asked me what the doctor said. I told her he had said I might have had a slight concussion, but it was basically just bumps and bruises. I said *he* said a good night's sleep should fix me up.

I went to bed before my parents started watching *Cheers*.

The next day, Friday, wasn't hugely different from the one before. My parents, it appeared, had decided to act "normal," but I knew that they were waiting. Waiting for me to ... *I* don't know, apologize in greater detail, or explain, and (surely) start behaving like their pride and joy again.

At school, I stalked through all my classes, still behind dark glasses. I hadn't done the work for any of them, but no teacher called on me, which meant that no one knew that but myself. Mr. Widmer handed back the Physics tests, and I got 82, the lowest grade I'd had all year. Ordinarily, I kept my tests and studied what I'd missed on them. This time, though, I left the damn thing lying on my desk, untouched, right where Mr. Widmer'd put it down.

A number of times during the day, I remembered I had made a date with Mary for that afternoon. One such time was when I got to Spanish class and found she wasn't there (and never did arrive, in fact). I think I kept remembering the date on purpose, taking a masochistic pleasure in the twisting of that recollection, playing hara-kiri with it, almost. Once or twice, I fantasized my going over to her house, just showing up, on schedule.

Of course I didn't, though. She could have the place "all to herself."

When I was in the barn that afternoon, the phone rang. If we knew my mom was home, we always let her pick it up inside the house; she got more calls than Dad, or Ben, the hired man, or me. When the call turned out to be for one of us, she pressed a buzzer that'd ring inside the barn.

This time, the buzzer buzzed. Ben was nearest, so he answered.

"For you," he called to me.

"Tell 'em I stepped out," I hollered back.

He shrugged and spoke into the phone, and hung it up.

About ten minutes later, when the two of us were close enough to speak in normal tones, he said to me, "When you get back from where you done stepped out to, you should—"

"I don't want to know who called," I interrupted him to say. "I don't want to speak to anyone."

"Suit yourself," he said, and went about his business.

The damn phone rang again at suppertime. This time I jumped up and told my mother that I didn't want to speak to anyone. I'd just leave the room, I said, in case it was for me; I also didn't want to know who called for me, I said.

When I came back in the room, both my parents stared at me.

"You're not speaking to *anyone* from school?" my father asked.

"That's correct," I said. "Not to any kids, and I don't think that any teachers or custodians will call. But if they do, I don't want to speak to them, either."

"And what, exactly, do you expect your mother and me to say to people who keep calling back for you?" he wondered.

"Anything you want," I said. "The most truthful thing would be, 'He doesn't want to speak to you.'"

"You're mad at everyone in the entire school?" my father asked, as if he didn't understand. As if he was some kind of *moron*.

I sighed. "Of course not," I said, phony-patiently. I didn't look at him. "I don't even know the names of half—three-quarters—of the kids down there. But *they're* not going to call me, are they? I just don't want to talk to any of the ones I know. Not now or any other day or night. Not ever."

"Oh, come on, dear," my mother said. "I know you're hurt and angry, but you mustn't let one incident, however unpleasant it may have been, destroy your senior year, the friendships that you've had *forever,* really. Now, Tara, just for instance, called and—"

"Tara," I said, interrupting, "is a perfectly nice person, who thinks very highly of both of you, I know. But she's moving to Boston next year and, to all intents and purposes, out of my life. That's typical of her, the kind of thing she does. To hell with her."

Even though my eyes were on my plate, I could see my parents' heads move as they looked at each other.

"You've been hurt, and you *are* hurt," my father said. "And so I sympathize with you, even if I don't know what the hell is going on. But as far as what you just said then, concerning Tara—well, I've gotta say you sounded like a jerk."

A noisy jumble filled my head, when he said that. I swear to God, I almost threw a punch at *him*. That's how mad I was.

Instead, I whispered to my mother, "May I be excused?" I knew my voice was out of my control.

"Yes," she said, "you may."

I left the table, ran up to my room, and locked the door. I

lay down on my bed, curled up, and closed my eyes. Things seemed to me to be in total chaos. There wasn't any aspect of my life I could take comfort in. I felt that I'd been sucked into a maelstrom; I was going down the drain. My mind, such as it was, was useless; it offered no ideas and no solutions, no escape route from the trap that I was in. I held my breath and vowed to keep it held until I came to a conclusion. But of course that didn't work; it never does.

19

SATURDAY morning, I didn't want to get out of bed. And when I did, I didn't want to leave my room.

But I knew I had to. I couldn't afford to get my parents—particularly my mother—too alarmed. I didn't want her getting any bright ideas. So, I went down and had breakfast while my father was in the barn, and I talked about my game plan for the day. I said I thought I'd haul our recyclables down to the Center in Burnside, and then stay and help out there awhile. Mom thought that was a *great* idea. And she wondered if, perhaps that afternoon, I'd like to drive with her to Dustin, to shop for a CD player. She said that she'd been thinking that we ought to have one in the house, that she'd read they were releasing a lot of "good stuff" on CD only, so probably the time had come . . . et cetera.

I said that, gee, I'd like to, but I couldn't. I said I had that major English paper coming due, and simply had to give a good chunk of the weekend to it. I didn't tell her that I didn't give a shit about CD's, or "good stuff," either. And that I'd decided, as a matter of fact, that the rock and roll community, in general, disgusted me. Take the Rolling Stones. From what I'd read, they used to be a lot like Gerry Mays and them, always screwing little teenaged girls. Bunch of goddamn predators, I thought.

But anyway—pretending I was going to the Recycling Center, I loaded the bed of the pickup with the bundled newspapers and flattened tin cans and well-rinsed glass bottles (clear and green and brown) and plastic detergent containers that we'd been saving for the past few weeks. I also put in our dump garbage, which was in a supposedly biodegradable plastic bag. At the last minute, I added my own contribution to its contents, most of the cassettes I owned. To hell with them, I thought, again. If my vinyl albums hadn't been so bulky, I would have taken them, too, probably.

Coming out of our dooryard, I turned toward town on Highridge Road, but when I got to Coffin's Hill, I didn't turn again; I kept on going straight. After about another four miles, I turned left onto Billups Hollow Road and went along its narrow gravel surface till I found the logging road that I was looking for. It angled steeply to the right, up through the trees. Having been created just the year before, it still was passable, if you went nice and easy over water bars, and skirted major ruts.

I did, for close to half a mile, I guess, then stopped, got out, and tossed the pickup's contents down the bank, which dropped off steeply to the right. Papers, bottles, cans, the trash—the works. It didn't make *too* big a mess, though one brown bag of papers did bust open, when it hit. No one but hunters ever came up there, I figured: I imagined they'd get blamed. And if they didn't like it, screw 'em. I'd had it with the kind of people I would have seen down at the Center, if I'd gone down there. A bunch of pompous, preachy, self-righteous tree-huggers—that was all they were.

When I was finished with unloading, I got back in the truck, turned the motor on, and cranked the heater up to high. The cab got warm real fast, with all the windows closed, so after a few minutes, I turned the motor off and just sat there. It stayed comfortable for a long time. I then got out again and walked around in the woods for a while, enjoying the quiet and the . . . privacy. A lot of people couldn't stand to be alone for periods of time, but I preferred it, actually. To be alone forever wouldn't be that bad, I thought.

All it'd take'd be some flexible two-inch plastic pipe—we had some in our shop, right by the barn—and run it from the exhaust into the cab of the truck, and then sit back and wait. That'd take care of everything. I'd never have to grovel and apologize to Tara, tell her what an utter, miserable idiot I'd been and ask her to forgive me all my trespasses and nastiness. And even more, I'd never ever have to wonder if I didn't *still* care mightily for Mary, even if she had refused me and betrayed me and preferred her really rotten slimeball bunch of other friends to me. Even if she'd partied her fool head off, while and after I was being nearly killed.

Three hours later, I drove home.

At lunch I chatted with my dad about the Giants' chances in the game they'd play against the Vikes the next day. And I told him I was sorry that I'd slept through morning milking. He told me, hey, no problem, that I ought to take it easy for a few days more. I could almost watch the guy relax, as I laid on the . . . normalcy.

My mother, during that same breaking of the bread (or, as it happened, hoagie rolls), handed me a bunch of slips from her phone message pad. You know, the kind that say *"While you were out _____ called at _____ Message: _____"* She said of course I didn't have to read them, but she confessed that she had had to fill them out, ever since the calls began. "Just as a common courtesy," she said; she couldn't bring herself to say I didn't want to talk to someone. She'd been saying she'd give me a message, she admitted. I just nodded as I took the things and shoved them in my right back pocket.

That afternoon I caught a lucky break. I was sitting at my desk, up in my room, supposedly working on that English paper (but actually canceling my subscription to *Time*), when out my window I observed a car pull up beside the house. It was Tara's mother's car, and T. herself got out of it. Of all the people that I couldn't face . . .

Quick as thought, I opened first my room door and then my other window, the one that gives onto the roof of our back porch. A moment later I was out of it (reclosing the window behind me), and sitting on the porch roof, with my back against the house. There, I couldn't be seen from anywhere, just about. I didn't move until I heard the car start up again and drive away.

At supper, Mom asked me real casually where I had gone that afternoon. I told her I'd been in my room for almost the entire time, except I *had* made one trip to the attic, where I'd gone to look for my old copy of *The Merchant of Venice*. And, while up there, I had seen some notebooks that I'd used way back in freshman year, and had got caught up in looking through them.

"Why'd you ask?" inquired this accomplished liar I'd become.

"Oh, no reason," she replied, and didn't look at me. Perhaps, I thought, this lying was contagious.

I was convinced, of course, that she'd asked Tara to come over. She handed me a couple more message slips, and I stuck them in the same back pocket.

"Will you be staying in tonight?" she asked offhandedly.

I could read her like ... a Shakespeare play. She was thinking that she might call Tara up again and try a rerun. She'd forgotten Tara worked at Angela's that night.

"I'm not sure yet," I said. "There's a movie down in Burnside that I'd like to see. I might hitch down and take it in. Tonight or tomorrow, I'm not sure. Tomorrow might be better, not as crowded."

"Oh, take my car," she said. "Whenever. Please. Feel free."

"Okay," I said. "I will."

And so I went up to my room, ostensibly to keep on plugging at that English paper. This time I actually did get out the start I'd made the week before, and read it through. The stuff I'd written seemed supremely ... unimportant. I balled the pages up and threw them at my wastebasket.

Oh, yes, of course I missed.

20

SUNDAY I told my mom I'd like to go to church with her again. Partly, I wanted to keep an eye on her. Partly, I knew I wouldn't run into Tara, or . . . other significant players in my former life. And partly, I had (imagine a self-mocking chuckle here) some "business" there.

I thought (ridiculous—or hopeless—as this possibly appears to you to be) I might get . . . guidance or advice at church. I hoped to hear or, better, *sense* what I should do, or not do, in the hours/days ahead.

Does this presumptuousness cause everyone to *gag*? Okay, okay—I know that not too many (any?) of the many thousand other people who attend religious services each week receive direct word from the Deity while they are sitting/standing/kneeling in their church or temple. Or, if they do, they sure don't talk about it. But still, it seemed to me I might.

And why? Why me? Well, that was it. Not for any *reason*—worthiness, especially—whatever. That's what's so wonderful about belief.

The only trouble was: Reality intruded, and I didn't get to church at all. Instead (and don't say "unbelievable"), I shoveled cow manure. Quite a contrast, eh? And not even our own cow manure—Uncle Elbie's!

What happened was, the barn cleaner up there, which does this same job automatically, mechanically, broke down.

And Elbie and his boys had driven down the night before to the Meadowlands, in New Jersey, where they had tickets to the Giants-Vikings game (almost everybody's for the Jints up here) that afternoon. Aunt May called up our house and talked to Mom, who told her she'd tell Dad when he came in from working on the sap-house he was building. That was a job he'd been trying to get to for a month or more.

When I'd realized that it was Aunt May, and not for me, I'd come back in the kitchen.

"What'd *she* want?" I asked Mom.

When I learned, I took the pickup and went up. I couldn't get the cleaner going—no one could, without a part that no one could've gotten on a Sunday—so I did the job by hand. Aunt May, who'd done the morning milking by herself already, babbled sentences of gratitude. I told her to forget it; I had always liked Aunt May. But I did accept her offer of a lunch, knowing that I wouldn't have to deal with anyone up there.

After I had eaten, I went home, but didn't stick around the house. I told my mother I was going for a walk and did.

We own considerable acreage, open land and wooded both, and through the years I'd found a lot of favorite spots on it, different, special "hideouts," as I thought of them. Some I'd chosen for their views, others on account of their locations by a fishing hole, or little waterfall; two were spacious, spreading oak trees that supported little "houses" I had made in them.

I visited each one, in turn, that day, and spent a little time with it, remembering. In a way, these places were the story of my life, my evolution; as a rule, each new one was a little more remote, a little farther from the house. But none of them was *now*, right then.

By the time I got back to the house again, I'd missed the

Giants game *and* the afternoon milking. I told my mother if her offer of the Buick was still good, I'd take her up on it and hit that movie that was playing downtown. And maybe catch a hot dog first, and bowl a few lines with whatever kids were hanging around the alleys. Mom said fine, by all means go ahead. But she didn't seem that thrilled, not in the best of moods. She handed me another message slip or two, which quickly joined the others, in my jeans.

I didn't do exactly what I'd said—not even close, in fact. Instead, I got a box of doughnuts and a soda at the Highridge Corners Store and went and parked up there off Burnt Hill Road, the place I'd parked with Mary.

I ate and drank and thought about my past, my present, and my future, sitting in the car. Each of them seemed stupid, bleak, or hopeless. I thought of being in the car that time with Mary, and I thought about the other times I'd been with her. I felt like puking up the doughnuts and the soda when I thought how possibly I could have *really* helped her, how I could have been a whole lot better player in her life (if I hadn't been a self-deluding fool)—how *both* of us had screwed up everything beyond belief, beyond all hope of changing it around again, so as to make it better. How I'd never end up, happily, with Tara now.

The whole damn trouble was: There wasn't anything to do that I *could* do, it seemed, to fix things up. Not with Tara, or with Mary, or with life in general.

I hadn't yet come to a . . . well, *conclusion*, though. Not quite; not yet. But I thought that I was getting closer; that it, bit by bit, was getting more . . . imaginable.

Put it this way: I was getting open to that possibility.

I sat there in the car till quarter after ten, and then drove home.

21

MONDAY morning, at our school, we have what's known as Assembly. You have to go to your homeroom first, where attendance is taken, but after that everyone—students, faculty, and staff—heads down to the varsity basketball court. That's where this Assembly is held.

Its alleged purpose is that tiresome old chestnut "school unity." Assembly is meant to "bring the school community together," and at least in a physical sense, it does. Spiritually, I'm not so sure. Mr. Reese, I've noticed, always tries to accentuate the positive in his remarks. He focuses on things that we've accomplished, both as a group and solo. Any team or individual that's done a halfway decent job the week before is apt to get a mention. Trophies and certificates are handed out; even *meals* ("... that *outstanding* home fried chicken last Tuesday ...") often have a moment in the sun. The cheerleaders are always front and center, to organize the rest of us, and our enthusiasm; oftentimes, the band plays, too. At the end, there are announcements of all sorts, many of them given by Mr. Lee, the vice-principal, but others by the student heads of clubs, or by faculty advisers.

I think they use the varsity basketball court for two reasons. First, noise is magnified in there, so you can seem to get a lot more enthusiasm going than in the older auditorium.

And second, because it *is* much newer, it also is a whole lot better looking. This basketball court—or wing, really—was actually *donated* to the school by Mr. and Mrs. Ed Hurlbut Sr. in 1985, in the afterglow of Burnside High's winning the State Basketball Championship for the first time since basketball was invented, whenever that was. Mr. Hurlbut was and is the president of the town's largest employer, Hurlbut Colonial Furniture, and Mrs. Hurlbut is principally the mother of Ed Hurlbut Jr., who averaged something like thirty-seven points a game as a forward for the Mountaineers during the '84–'85 season. I believe she dressed in green and gold at every game, home and away, that year.

The Hurlbut Arena, as this thing is known, was made to be used as the site for the Southern Regional Play-offs, which lead to the State Championship game (which is always played at the University, a neutral site for everyone). That's why it's as big and fancy as it is.

What you have to imagine is permanent stands along both sides of the court and at each end, behind the baskets. Spectators gain access to these stands through lockable double doors—six sets of them, in all—which are located at the top of both sides of the stands. These give onto a sort of a wide walkway that goes around the entire arena. A lot of sets of stairs go down from it, between the different sections of the stands, right down to the floor.

The players and officials reach the court from locker rooms, which are located underneath the stands, and that's where the principal, the vice-principal, the cheerleaders, and any other celebrities on the morning program come from. In preparation for Assembly, the custodial staff unrolls some narrow strips of rubber matting, which run from the locker-room area toward the center of the basketball court itself. There, a large green and gold rug, made out of indoor-outdoor carpeting, has been laid down, and in the middle of it there's a microphone on a stand. That's hooked into the permanent speaker system, which hangs there over mid-court, aimed in all directions.

I walked briskly, and alone, from my homeroom to the Hurlbut, and I took a seat in the back row, on one side. The seats are bleacher-style—in other words, wide maple boards, held up by metal pipes set into concrete. They are hard and uncomfortable, and encourage people to stand up and cheer a lot. At least in the very last row, where I was, you can lean back against the little wall that runs along the back of every section.

My mood was pretty much as it had been. I didn't know what I was doing, there at school. Oh, I still knew that school was like a springboard into college, but if a person didn't want to go to college (anymore), it wasn't anything except a place to pass one's time. Just like college was, when you got right down to it. Of course, it was also probably true that lots of kids found both school *and* college to be pleasant, in a way. They could hang around with other kids their age, and get some sort of bang from their . . . *relationships*. That hardly was the case with me, however. At its best, school was now a sort of a diversion, a place that possibly might take my mind off other things. What other things? you ask. Try this: the fact that *anything* I did—whether it was school, college, or working on a farm—would merely be a thing to take my mind off other things.

Soon after I came in, the band also entered the arena and sat in the section reserved for it, down and to the right of where I was. Shortly afterward, the principal, vice-principal, and cheerleaders, accompanied by the bandmaster, the boys' and girls' varsity soccer coaches, and the English teacher who's adviser to the Drama Club, walked out onto the green and gold carpet and milled about informally.

I stared at them, these featured players. I knew all their names. Over half of them knew mine, I guessed, though none of them knew *me*.

But—*Tilt!* Hey, what the hell . . . (I thought). *Mary* wasn't there, wearing her white sweater with the big green *B* on it, standing on the carpet, showing off, and chatting with her fellow cheerleaders, her group, her chosen friends. I wondered where she was. I'd seen her from behind at Spanish class, four days before, on Thursday morning; she hadn't looked herself. Then, later on that day, I'd seen her standing on the steps with Tara, deep in conversation. And now that I thought about it, she hadn't looked herself on that occasion, either. They'd been standing close together, Mary with her head down, and Tara'd had ahold of her, her *hand,* the way a girl will do who's *comforting* another girl who's sick or something. Or in this case, possibly, hung over.

Then, Friday, Mary hadn't been in school at all—or hadn't been at Spanish class, in any case. Probably, she'd cut—and then had had another blast on Saturday, recuperated Sunday, and then cut again today. I guessed that pretty much took care of that "new Mary" she had told me she was starting out to be, as far as schoolwork went. Pretty clearly, I'd had no effect on her, whatever.

Most of the kids and teachers and staff members had arrived by then. There were still a whole lot of empty seats in the arena, but that was always the case; it was big enough to hold at least two schools the size of ours. With nothing else to do, I sent my eyes around the gym.

And—yikes! There came Mary Sutherland and Tara, walking along together on the gym floor, directly in front of the first row of the side stands, right below me. As they passed center court, one of the cheerleaders on the carpet—it might have been that Amy Golden—looked at them and said something, but neither of them turned to answer. They kept on walking until they got to the end stands, right behind the basket, and then they both sat down there, in the first row. I couldn't help but notice that Gerry Mays and a few of his friends were also sitting in that section, higher up, and that one of them tossed *something*—it could have been a piece of doughnut, or a crumpled notebook page—down in the direction of the two girls. It landed in the row behind them, which was mostly empty, but all the guys hee-hawed like crazy, anyway. And Tara leaned over close to Mary and said something in her ear. I thought Mary looked . . . well, *smaller* than before, sitting in her blue jean jacket and dark pants, with her shoulders rounded and her clasped hands resting on her knees.

I shifted on my seat. It surely *was* uncomfortable; I shifted once again. That made me realize I was even more uncomfortable than . . . than, well, I *had to* be. I reached into my right back pocket and pulled out the stack of papers from my mother's message pad. (That's right, I don't change blue jeans very often.) My eyes fell on the topmost one.

"While you were out . . ." I read—and kept on reading, this time.

The one on top was a surprise. The caller was Dwayne Delbert, and the message was: "Be sure to be in that Assembly on Monday." Though it was clear enough, that made no sense, whatever. Did Dwayne expect to get some kind of prize? Or did he think *I* was in line for one? Well, here I was. I had got the message and, although unwittingly, I'd acted on it. Maybe all the other messages would prove to be as totally irrelevant, I thought. Maybe all of them would have as much effect on me as I had had on Mary Sutherland.

But the others were from Tara—all but two of them—and I read them over and over, and over again. The Assembly program started. Different ones said this and that. Cheers were cheered and the band played, and if anything good was said about Dwayne, I missed it. I just kept on leafing through those messages, pretty well spaced out.

No wonder Mom had started looking at me strangely. What Tara'd told her to put down, at first, was not so bad— brisk, but unenlightening. Along the lines of "Give me a ring," and "Please call *now*." But soon she got more forceful: "Stop doing this—there's stuff you need to know," that kind of thing. The last bunch, though, were mostly questions: "Do you even know what Mary did at Gerry's mother's *after*?" and "Do you even *care* what anybody else is thinking, feeling, needing?" and "Why are you being so awful?" The very final one said, "I can't wait until I've seen the last of you."

There were also two slips that had Mary's name on them. Her calls had come on Friday afternoon and night, and in the part for Message, Mom had written "None."

All I could think, as I kept fingering those slips, was that, incredibly, the mess I'd helped to make was even bigger than I'd thought it was.

I imagine that my eyes took in the unfamiliar movement on the court in front of me, but at first it didn't register in my brain. Not until I heard the voice from down there; it got through to me at once. Perhaps it was its incongruity. Mr.

Reese and Mr. Lee and the other teachers have a certain way of talking. I don't know if they sound "educated," or "out of state," or what. But they sure as hell don't sound like High-ridge Road, the way that this guy did.

"Everybody stay right in their seats," he said. "Them exit doors are all chained shut."

The voice belonged to Davey Delbert, Dwayne and Dwight's old man, and he was standing down there on that carpet, holding a rifle in one hand and the microphone in the other. The mike was a little closer to his mouth than it had to be, and he was sort of bent forward at the waist, as if he was afraid the thing might drip on him. He was dressed about as usual: dark green work pants, scuffed-up leather boots, a flannel shirt and insulated vest. On his head, a John Deere baseball cap. Davey was a logger—most days, anyway.

Four other Delberts, armed the same as him—three of Davey's brothers, along with his son Dwight—were also on the carpet. They seemed capable of making it quite clear to Mr. Reese and all of them that they shouldn't interfere with the proceedings.

"No innocent parties is gonna get hurt. Most all you folks are here as witnesses, not players. If everybody just stays sittin' in their seats . . ."

By this time, it had started to sink in, to everyone, that Davey and his kinfolk weren't part of any "program," and that something untoward and maybe hazardous was fixing to take place. People had turned their heads to look back at the exit doors, and some of them had seen the chains on them, with other rifle-toting Delberts up there, quite nearby. Some "witnesses" stood up. A lot of kids and teachers started talking.

So, Davey brought his rifle barrel up and, shooting from

the hip, he fired a round right through the glass basketball backboard in front of him. A million starburst cracks appeared in it, and the bullet buried itself in the ceiling.

The explosion—magnified in that environment—had a real effect. After some scattered cries of "Oh, my God" and such, everyone shut up, except for some who tried to muffle sobs. Those who'd gotten up had sat back down again.

"That's a whole lot better," Davey Delbert said, and cleared his throat. "These other men and me are here so justice can get done. When it is, you'll all be free to go about your business." Dwight and his three uncles were now standing on the four corners of the court, looking up into the stands—for troublemakers, I supposed. They held their rifles at "port arms," across their chests. I figured that, except for Dwight, they'd all been in the service, over in Vietnam.

"Now then," continued Davey. "The thing that got us here is that two weeks ago my son Dwayne Delbert was beat up on by a teacher here. It was an unfair fight. That teacher is still workin' at this school; he ain't been fired, or nothin'. So today, them two—this teacher and my son—is gonna fight again, but fair. And all of you are gonna see who beats."

He turned and looked toward one of the locker-room doors, and Dwayne came out of it, on cue. He was dressed good, in a nice slim pair of light tan corduroy jeans, and a kind of a cream-colored western shirt, and that old cowboy hat of his, and cowboy boots that weren't new but had a good, bright shine on them. Around his waist he wore a gun belt, with a quick-draw buscalero holster on it, and that Ruger that he'd shown me sticking out of it.

And in one hand, he had another gun belt, with another shiny holstered pistol.

"Now, let's hold on a minute, here."

That was Mr. Lee, the vice-principal. One of his main jobs was keeping order in the school, I guess. He was in charge of discipline, so he was used to telling people what to do and where to go, or else. He took a step toward Davey Delbert, and he looked quite cross. The foolish man believed that he was still in charge.

I imagine he didn't know much about loggers in general, though, and even less about Davey. A lot of guys who work in the woods—who do that cold, hard, dangerous work called logging—are the sort of people who don't take to being bossed around. That's one reason they went into the woods to begin with; loggers are pretty much their own boss. People say that Davey Delbert has mellowed a lot, since he was a kid. Once upon a time, apparently, he'd start a fight if you looked cross-eyed at him. And even today, he's not the kind of man you'd want to give a lot of guff to.

"Davey's a good man and a hard worker," I had heard my dad say once. "But he can still get awful tetchy sometimes—so I understand."

Well, I suppose that this was "sometimes." He put the microphone that he'd been holding back there on its stand. He had the rifle in his left hand still, with a finger on the trigger guard, but it was tilted backward, resting on his shoulder.

"Shut up, you," he said to Mr. Lee, and he slapped him on the side of his head with that big right paw of his, a hand that usually was wrapped around the handle of a heavy chainsaw, or getting tow chain on a big old log, or working the controls of some high-tired yellow skidder.

The upper half of Mr. Lee went left, and his feet didn't move fast enough to stay under it, so down he sprawled, on the carpet. He wasn't really hurt, and so was able to roll right into a sitting position, with his left hand feeling for his face. But he didn't try to get back on his feet, and he absolutely did shut up.

"The rest of you sit down by him," said Davey to the principal, the bandmaster, the two coaches, the theatrical director, and the cheerleaders. "Right over on the edge of that there carpet." They did as they were told.

I've no idea if Mr. Lee had guessed what was about to happen. I didn't have to guess; I knew. So, I stood up and started down the steps. I remembered Dwayne had called the kids at school "the boys," and "rotten sonsabitches." He wouldn't care what happened to them, even accidentally.

I hadn't gone three steps before the shot came. It was fired by one of Dwayne's uncles on the floor, not Dwight or Davey, and it went a little bit over my head and into the woodwork above one of the chained doors.

I stopped. I can't say I braced myself for the next shot; I just stopped. Maybe he had *meant* to miss me. I didn't *want* to die, not then, but if I did, well, fine.

I could see that Dwayne was speaking to his father, but of course I couldn't hear the words.

Davey put the microphone back by his lips again.

"*You* can keep on going, Shepherd," Davey's voice boomed out. "Dwayne says that you can leave, if you've a mind to, although he wishes you would stay." He cleared his throat again. "But everybody else stays absolutely put, y'understand? Nobody move, a-tall."

I felt a lot of eyes switch onto me as I walked down the steps and onto the basketball floor. Perhaps, for once, a lot of people wished that they were me. But me, instead of turning toward the locker room, I headed for the end stands, to my left. Tara and Mary watched me coming, seated side by side there in Row 1, with no one else beside them or in back of them. I thought that Tara looked surprised and on her guard; Mary took one peek, saw that it was me, and dropped her head, staring at the floor between her feet.

"Please," I said, not loudly, looking straight in Tara's eyes. "Please—dear God—I know what's going to happen, and I'm *begging* you. If you'd just move, up in the second row, right close behind her." And I nodded at the back of Mary's lowered head, but with my eyes locked into Tara's still. *"Please."*

She didn't move for probably a count of five. I had the feeling she was looking way inside my brain, and possibly my heart as well. One thing I could count on, anyway: Tara knew me—knew me, maybe, even better than I knew myself. At last she nodded, shrugged, and did what I had asked her to.

I turned and faced the center of the gym. The backs of both my calves were almost touching Mary's knees. It would be hard for either one of them to see, but that was not the point of all of this, their seeing or not seeing everything that happened. The point was: I was in the way.

Now, I thought; so, *now.*

Dwayne looked at me and touched his hat brim briefly, and I thought he nodded, too. Then he strolled on over to the far side stands, where Mr. Melchiorre was sitting in the fourth row. In spite of Davey's warning, people in the first three rows squinched left and right a little, so the two of them were face to face, with no one in between.

Dwayne held out the extra gun belt and said something.

Melchiorre answered something back, and Dwayne took his Ruger out of its holster, slowly and deliberately, then cocked it with his thumb and shot it into the space between the teacher's shins. After that, he raised the barrel of his pistol up a little higher and said something else.

Mr. Melchiorre rose and came down from the stands, and

followed Dwayne out on the carpet. He took off his jacket, folded it, and laid it on the floor. Then he took the gun belt and buckled it around his ample waist. Dwayne said something else, and so he bent and got his tie-down looped around his thigh—you know, that leather thong that comes out from the bottom of a holster, holding it in place.

Dwayne spoke still another time. I guessed that he was giving Melchiorre the choice of ends, going by the way the teacher looked around. He finally lumbered toward the far end of the carpet, where he turned to face in our direction. Dwayne put his back to us and, eyes on Melchiorre, took about four backward steps and stopped.

"You can draw and fire any time now, gentlemen," said Davey Delbert, through the microphone.

There was a sudden sound from farther up behind me: footsteps clumping down on bleacher seats, a muttered curse. Two guys had realized what was happening, I guess: that a big old Phys. Ed. teacher, also ex-marine (or soldier, anyway), was getting set to shoot a gun more or less in their direction. So, no matter what they'd just been told, they were bailing out, and fast.

A Delbert uncle moved to intercept them as they reached the floor, not that far from me. He thrust his rifle butt into the first boy's gut, then swung it up against the second's neck. They went down like two pins on that shiny maple surface, Gerry Mays and Tipper Doane, overmatched this time. I smiled at them; I couldn't help myself. They lay there, dazed and fearful, looking toward the floor.

I suppose that Mr. Melchiorre figured here was his best chance—to get a first shot in while Dwayne was all distracted by the ruckus. He made a frantic grab for his revolver.

I think that pleased D. Wayne. I'm pretty sure that, all along, he'd planned to spot the guy first move—and there it was. So, much faster than I possibly could put the words together, describing what he did, he snatched that Ruger out and started fanning it. (That "fanning" is pure quick-draw stuff, the fastest way to cock and fire.)

Five shots rang out, so close together you could hardly count them, echoing in that arena. Melchiorre never got one off. In fact, he fumbled his damn gun while he was pulling it, and dropped it on the floor right by his feet.

Well. My first thought was: that *Dwayne!*—that crazy, smartass . . . *Highridge Road-er!* I wasn't going to have to stop a bullet after all; there weren't any bullets! A normal person would have been relieved, I guess. I suppose I *was* relieved. But maybe I was disappointed, too. I honestly can't say.

I turned and looked at Tara and at Mary.

"Shepherd, you big jerk," said Tara. "You thought they had live ammo, didn't you?" I think I nodded at her; I'm not sure. I turned back toward the center of the room.

The Phys. Ed. teacher, big bull that he was, was swaying on his feet, his face contorted. I could see a dark stain spreading down the right leg of his khaki pants.

Dwayne, by then, had spun the Ruger back into its holster. He walked across the rug to Mr. Melchiorre, jerked the gun belt off his waist, and scooped up his revolver from the floor. The microphone, now back up on its stand, picked up the words he said.

"Wet your pants there, sucker?"

Then, moving quickly and surrounded by his kinfolk, D. Wayne Delbert, resident of Highridge Road, walked out of the arena.

I knew, the same as he and all the other Delberts did, I'm sure, that there'd be heavy consequences. People can't walk into public high schools, even in Vermont, with rifles, and shoot holes in walls and backboards. Kids can't force teachers into gunfights in gymnasiums, even when the whole thing is a fake, and nobody gets hurt—even when they're getting even for injustice. Yep, there'd be hell to pay, all right, but I could—and *would*, sure—testify about what Melchiorre did to Dwayne, to start all this.

Now, the teacher seemed to be in shock. His head was down, and shaking, and he had his hands up in the air in front of him, as if he was a surgeon, waiting for his gloves. Taking little mincing steps, he edged toward Mr. Reese, and I could see his lips were moving. The principal looked somewhat sympathetic, but not totally supportive. He brushed right by his Phys. Ed. teacher, reaching for the microphone.

Everybody must have realized by then that Melchiorre didn't have a gunshot wound. No one had been shot. Dwayne had had just one real bullet in his Ruger—the one he'd shot between the teacher's legs to make him leave the stands. All the rest were blanks. I just assumed that Melchiorre's gun had *only* blanks in it, but hell, you never know.

Mr. Reese had trouble getting anyone's attention. He was urging all the students and the teachers and the staff members to sit back down and come to order. But that was not to be. Everybody wanted to blow out of there. The Delberts had unchained the upper entryways, along both sides, and people started exiting through them, instead of trying to push their way down to the floor, and go out through the locker rooms, as D. Wayne and his dad had done.

I took my time, but when I saw that it was open, I headed for the door that I'd come in by—who knows why. Gerry Mays and Tipper Doane were sitting up when I went by them, and I think one of them spoke to me. I had no plan of where to go, or what to do.

I began to climb the stairs, oblivious to everyone around me. It seemed that now I'd totally run out of things to do. Assembly was over. I hadn't done the work for any of my classes. I'd taken care of all the things I had to do up home. The only thing that I could think to do was *move*—keep on going, off, away from where I was, and go and go until I reached . . . whatever. The limits of my patience, maybe—*I* don't know. I thought I heard a siren in the distance.

There was a lot of high-pitched babble in the hall, outside of the arena. People seemed to need to share what they had seen with one another. I could tell that I was being looked at as I kept on going down the corridor, heading for a door to the outside.

I didn't hear them coming. So, when they got their arms around me, one on either side, I gave a jump, a start.

How could this possibly be happening? I thought, as they leaned into me. And then I finally started crying, just accepting it, and hugged them back.

Days before, I'd started on what could have been a fatal spin, much like the kind that happens—well, *can* happen—if you're in a car and drive too fast onto a patch of hard black ice. You find yourself just going, knowing you have no control; uh-oh, you say, this time I may have *really* done it.

Then, by some miracle, you get your traction back; you're saved. You hardly can believe it, but you surely can accept it. You may even cry.

There seemed to be a lot of noise, confusion, in my head.

But also Tara saying, "Shepherd, you big *jerk*. You *love*. You *sweetheart!*"

And Mary sobbing, "Sorry, sorry, sorry."

You want to hear the most amazing consequence of all of this?

It's not that the little rift between my parents and myself is all patched up; that was bound to happen, anyway. And it's not even that Tara's decided to move to Burlington (where I will be) instead of Boston in the fall—which means that I can tell her constantly and face-to-face how much I love and want and need her. All it took for that to happen was for me to stop being one kind of a jerk and get back to being an honest one.

No, the most amazing outcome is that Mary and my folks—especially my mom—have gotten to be close. Tara fixed that up, of course. She told me Mary needed Mom—but also vice-versa, I discovered.

"Oh, I was *dreading* it," I heard my mother say to Mary on the phone, one day, "having Shep away at college. Having nobody around that I could pester and abuse like I do him. I thought I'd wither away. And then, what happens? *You* show up, and pretty soon I've got if not the daughter, well, at least the *niece* I always wanted, never had. I swear," she said to Mary, "I believe you're going to save my life!"

Aha, I thought. The mystery is finally solved. It wasn't me but Mary that my favorite band was talking to.

Or was it?

ABOUT THE AUTHOR

Julian F. Thompson is the author of ten books for young adults, among them *The Grounding of Group 6*, *A Band of Angels*, *Gypsyworld*, and *The Fling*.

He and his wife, Polly, divide their time between Burlington and West Rupert, Vermont.